Homebound

HAYLEY ANDERTON

For Jack - the person who sees me through every single obstacle. I love you.

OTHER BOOKS BY HAYLEY ANDERTON

All books are available to purchase as paperbacks or ebooks. All books are also enrolled in Kindle Unlimited.

Apocalypse Series

Book 1: Apocalypse
Book 2: Fallout
Book 3: Chaos
Book 4: Sacrifice
Book 5: Outlast

The Last Girls on Earth Series

Book 1: Sloth
Book 2 : Gluttony

Coming Soon…
The Risen Series

Book 1: The Risen
Book 2: The Lost
Book 3: The Remains

When one door closes, another one opens.

OUTSIDE

There's a lot resting on a birthday wish. You only get them once a year, and you don't want to waste them. Sure, you get other opportunities in the year to make a wish. A turkey bone at Christmas, four leaf clovers, dandelion puffs and shooting stars. But birthday wishes are the best. They actually work sometimes.

"Make a wish, Lori!" Marigold tells me as I sit in front of my cake, seventeen candles wedged into the icing. The whole kitchen smells of burning sugar as the wax melts onto the cake. Marigold and Rita wait expectantly with their hands entwined, proud parents on their daughter's birthday. Rowena sits with her clunky boots up on the chair next to her, eyeing up the cake from the corner of her eye. Honey's bent over her homework, her long hair a curtain that almost covers her face, but she's smiling, humming Happy Birthday.

"Come on, Lori, you'll be eighteen before you make a wish at this rate," Rowena says, rolling her eyes. I chew my thumb.

"I've not thought of one yet."

"Birthday wishes are for babies," she mutters, chipping at her black nail varnish. Since she turned thirteen last month, she's become the model example of why old people hate teenagers. But she won't spoil this for me. This is a good day, and I won't rush on her account.

"Don't listen. Take your time," Honey murmurs so only I can hear, but she doesn't look up from her homework. I squeeze my eyes shut. I don't care what Ro says anyway. Wishes do come true sometimes, and they're not just for kids. A birthday wish got me here – here with a family. Eight years ago, I started wishing that a family would take me in and love me the way I've always wanted to be loved. Two years later, that came true.

What can I wish for when I have everything now? Over the years, my wishes have slowly come true – to get fostered, to be loved by a family, then adopted. But now I have all of those things. I could wish for my constant anxiety to disappear, but wishes aren't miracles. So what do I want? I take a deep breath and blow out the candles.

I wish for everything to stay the same.

Marigold claps softly and rests her blushed cheek against Rita's as I blow out my candles. I hang my head to hide my smile. Rita and Marigold both bend to put their arms around me from behind. I can feel Rita's curls and Marigold's long, beaded necklaces tickling my face. Rita pecks my cheek.

"Our little girl. Seventeen…"

I'm practically glowing. It always makes me feel good when they call me their daughter, or their little girl. Rowena would die if she received the same treatment, but then again, she was never as desperate to leave the care system as I was. I know some people my age are desperate to escape the affections of their parents, but not me. I'm making up for lost time.

Rita straightens up, her arms re-twining around her wife.

"Right then. Birthday presents? Check. Birthday cake? Check. What else?"

"Birthday pizza?" Marigold smiles.

Rita holds up a finger as though she's hit a eureka moment. "I knew we'd forgotten something. What does everyone want?"

"Pepperoni!" Honey and I cry in unison. She finally glances up from her work to smile at me.

Rowena folds her pale, skinny arms.

"I'm not eating pizza. I'm on a diet."

Rita moves to place her hands firmly on Rowena's shoulders. "No you're not, darling. What have I told you a million times?"

Rowena sighs. "That diet culture is a torture tactic invented by men to control women."

"And what else?"

"That pizza once in a while is just as healthy as eating your seven a day," Rowena recites monotonously. "But I don't even like pizza."

"You did the last time we ate it…"

"Well not anymore."

Marigold sighs. "Do you have to be so difficult, Ro?"

Rita shoots Marigold a dark look and Marigold sits at the table, biting her tongue. I sit back and watch Rita work her magic. She puts a finger under Rowena's chin gently, tilting it up.

"You know I won't force you to do anything you don't want to do. But I also think that since it's Lori's birthday, we can both afford to let loose a little, hmm? What about a veggie supreme to share, my dear?"

A ghost of a smile flickers on Ro's sullen face for a moment, before it's replaced with a sour expression. "Sure. Whatever." Where Rowena's concerned, that's got to be a win.

Rita grins, ruffling Rowena's black bobbed hair. Ro's hands immediately rush to smooth it back down. Rita crosses to the other side of our circular dinner table and closes Honey's textbook. Honey looks up, panic-stricken.

"Enough studying for now, Honey."

"But-"

"No buts. You've been working all day, a couple of hours off won't kill you. What do I always say?"

Honey rolls her eyes with an affectionate smile."That all work and no play means no one is sticking it to The Man?"

"Precisely. Go and pick out a film. Lori and I are going to get the pizzas, so have something ready to go for when we get back."

Honey bites her lip, her face half hidden behind her pale hair as she glances at me. "Sorry. I didn't mean to be a buzzkill. I just have so much work to do…"

I nod, but I'm not really concentrating. All I can think is about what Rita just said. That we're going out to get the pizza. I swallow back the lump in my throat.

"Can't I stay here and help choose the film? Please?" I blurt, interrupting Honey. Rita and Marigold exchange a glance. Marigold makes herself busy by heading into the kitchen, refusing to look at me on her way. Rita raises an eyebrow at me.

"Come on. Get your coat."

"Pretty birthday please?" I joke, but I'm hoping she'll change her mind. My palms are clammy with sweat. My heart tries to find rhythm but stays just slightly off beat. Rita shakes her head, knowing my ploy.

"Lori, we're going. Now."

A familiar nausea starts to bubble inside me. The last thing I want to do is go outside. Our family doesn't have a car which means we'll have to get the bus. It's rush hour, we'll be stuck between dozens of strangers. They'll crowd my space. Suffocate me. I don't want to. I can't. But I don't say no to Rita. Not now, not ever.

Ten minutes later, we're set to leave. Mari pecks Rita on the lips as we head for the door, then plants a kiss on my cheek, filling me with warmth. It makes me forget my nerves for a moment. Marigold fiddles with her long hair, smiling as she weaves the dark strands into tiny plaits.

"Don't forget garlic bread," she says. Rita rolls her eyes affectionately.

"As if you'd let us forget. We'll be back in an hour, tops. Come on, my darling."

This is the moment I can't deal with. The moment where we have to step out of the warmth and comfort of the house. We have to go down the driveway and out into the street and then cross the road to the bus stop. I stare out at the dark road. Anything can happen out there, at night. It's worse out here when the sky darkens. In town, there will be drunks darting in and out of the pubs, and taxis weaving through traffic, and crowds of people laughing as they bustle past. People will be staring at me, wondering what my problem is and why I can't just have fun like the rest of them. Seventeen is meant to be the age where people go out drinking and kissing strangers at parties. Or as far as I know. These are the things I never plan to do. I just want to stay where I feel safe.

Every opportunity, though, Rita insists on dragging me out of the house with her. We could have ordered in tonight. Mari prepared afternoon tea at the house earlier so we wouldn't have to go out. But Rita is intent on pushing me to my limits. She does it for my own good, I know that. But it makes me hate my favourite person in the world a little bit each time she makes me do this.

My foot hovers in the space between our hallway and the stone step outside. My whole body trembles. My foot dips onto the step for a moment before I retract it, as though I've plunged my toes in freezing water. Cold rushes through my heart, through my veins. I stumble back into the hall, breathing hard. Marigold sighs in sympathy, but steps away to allow Rita to handle me.

Rita edges around me to stand on the step outside. Her face isn't really sympathetic, but it's kind. In some ways, it's inviting. She's not worried about me. She believes I can do this.

"Remember what I told you?" she asks. Her gruff voice has raised an octave.

I nod. We created a mantra together to help me push through my anxiety attacks. *I am loved. I am supported. I will not be left alone.* The next part I add myself.

I can do this.

But my body disagrees. As I step outside, I can feel my pulse raising. Blood thumps in my head. Constant, a metronome. My fingers go numb. I stagger forwards, dazed. Rita takes my elbow and marches me away. My lungs shudder as we walk. I try to focus. What's the situation? Where are we going?

Goal number one. Bus stop. It can't be more than twenty metres away. I can do it. *No, I can't.* I pause and

Rita's hand slips from my elbow. I'm alone. I gasp in the time it takes Rita to retake my arm. She taps under my chin, making me raise my head.

"Deep breath. Keep going."

I carry on, breathless like an out of practice runner. But I concentrate on my lungs, forcing them to do their job. After an eternity, my eyes refocus and my hand brushes the cold, yellow metal of the bus stop. I drum my fingers on the glass of the stand. I can hear Rita saying something to me, but I can't make sense of her words. My breathing comes in sharp, shallow gasps. But I can feel Rita's hand, soft and gentle, on my shoulder. I focus on her touch and the warmth of her palm. The boniness of her metal rings on my skin. And suddenly, it's a little easier to breathe again.

As I calm down, I'm able to refocus on the world around me. Sometimes my panic attacks take me so far out of this world that it takes a few minutes to re-familiarise myself with it all. The street is quiet – we're the only two people at the bus stop. I sigh in relief. I try to swallow the lump in my throat, desperate to focus on other things. I watch a street light flicker into life, emitting a low buzzing noise as it spills amber light onto the pavement. If I look at it for long enough, I can pretend I'm back in my bedroom, where my orange lampshade casts a glow over everything. I'm not standing out in the cold, out in the street. I'm home.

Until Rita pulls me from my thoughts by wrapping her arms around me. Still, I feel safer knowing she's beside me. I bury my face into her. She smells of lavender, and lavender smells of home.

"You know I'm doing this for your own good, don't you?"

I sigh, nodding into her chest. "I know."

"You don't have to talk. I know it's not easy for you to be out in public. But you can do this. You're doing great."

As I pull away, I try for a smile. Rita has done a lot to help me over the past few years. When my anxiety is at its worst, she helps me through it. But when I'm doing okay, she tries to help me work past it. She doesn't want me to hide in the house forever. She wants me to have a life. It's hardest for me - Honey is Rita's biological daughter, and she inherited her unwavering courage. Rowena might be adopted too, from a background as dark as my own, but she's filled with fire and passion for life. She has no intention of hiding away. But one glance back at the life I've lived so far, the things I've suffered before I even turned seventeen, and I feel my strength crumble. Every single time.

But that's why Rita pushes me so hard. She knows that I want to stay hidden away in the house where I feel like I'm untouchable. But she also knows that's no way to live.

"A temporary solution is not a solution at all," Rita tells me now. "It's like putting a plaster on a gun-shot wound. That's why we have to get through this and put it behind you. Not just wade through the mud all the time. It might feel impossible, but it's not. I know you have it in you."

I try to hold on to that thought. Rita's hand returns to my shoulder, her grip firm, but not in a bad way. It makes me feel like she'll hold me up even if my legs fail me. Then the bus comes into view and I seize up. Rita's hand feels ghostly, distant. But I can still hear her voice. I cling to it with all my might.

"Remember what I taught you." It's not a question this time. It's a demand.

I am loved. I am supported. I will not be left alone. I repeat it, over and over and over. My legs shake as we step onto the bus, but I repeat the mantra as we take the last empty seats near the back. Furthest from the door. Furthest from the escape. I grip the seats, thinking of how many things could go wrong on here. We could crash and there are no seatbelts to stop us from flying off in one direction or another. Someone on the bus could be violently ill and infect us all. I dig my fingernails into my palm. Worst case scenarios have become the specialty of my troubled mind over the years.

But Rita won't let me dwell on them. She fishes her ancient iPod out of her pocket and hands me a headphone. I repeat my mantra again as Rita lets me pick the music. I select her old band, listening to the husk of her voice singing in my ear as we ride the bus. I rest my head against her shoulder, shutting the world out. If I close my eyes, I don't notice if people stare at me. I can disappear.

I am loved. I am supported. I will not be left alone.

I hear Rita rustling around in her pocket and she holds out a bag of sour gummy sweets to me. I try for a smile and take one. Rita read somewhere that tasting something sour can bring you back down to Earth when you're having an anxiety attack. Something about it being a shock to the system. Sometimes it helps, sometimes it doesn't. But I'm grateful for the effort. I put a sweet in my mouth and savour it as the bus trundles along.

It's a relief when the bus stops again and Rita nudges me to stand up. We step off into the cold street and I take a deep breath of fresh air. We're close enough to the centre of town that I can hear the bustle of people, but far enough away that we're safe from it. In the distance, a police siren wails, but it's far away. We're okay here. Rita loops her arm through mine. She smiles at me.

"Okay?"

I nod. I feel okay. Rita squeezes my arm and we carry on walking towards our favourite pizza takeaway. I'm alert and scanning the street for possible obstacles. People, mainly. But I can hear Rita talking about a reunion with her band friends, and I manage to respond appropriately to her and ask all the right questions. Soon enough, I can see the takeout sign across the road, glowing neon in the dark.

Goal three.

There are a group of young boys hanging outside, their hoods pulled over their heads. They laugh and I'm sure it's at me. I know it is. I take a step back, stiff. Rita pulls me a little closer. I can hear the distant police siren getting closer. I feel like it's in my head, screaming *danger! danger!* My legs are trembling so much that I know if I move, I'll fall.

No. That's not true. Rita wouldn't let me. Her arm acts as my spine, holding me up.

"They won't bother you. They're just a group of friends hanging out together. They don't care about what we're doing."

I nod to let her know I'm listening. It embarrasses me, the way she has to talk me through every step of our journey. Without her guidance, I would never have made it this far. I would barely have made it off the doorstep. But everything feels wrong. Sometimes, it feels so wrong to fight my instincts that I don't even want to try. But I do. I try because Rita wants me to.

And after everything we've been through, I want to do this for her.

Rita tugs me and I shuffle after her, reluctant. I stare at the shop ahead – the goal. I swallow the lump in my throat. *You're almost there. You can do this.*

Rita turns her attention back to me, smiling. "I'm starving. I bet I'll eat it all before we get-"

Tyres skid around the corner. A siren wails. There's a car headed for us. Too fast. Rita's head whips round. Her face falls. Her eyes lock mine as she shoves me hard. I fall backwards, reaching for her to catch me.

My back hits the floor.

There's a sound like a football hitting a window. I sit up as the car hits the lamppost. It crumples to half its size. On impact, it sounds like knives and forks clashing in a crockery drawer.

For a few seconds, there's silence. I blink. Once. Twice. The world comes into focus.

Rita is limp in the middle of the road. I stumble to my feet, backing away. Someone grabs my arms, too hard. Trying to tug me away. I resist. I need to get closer. All I can see is Rita, her blonde curls covering her face. Her legs at strange angles.

Someone is saying something to me, but their voice is just a buzz. The boys in hoods rush into the road. Crowding Rita, hiding her from me. I try to get to her, but someone holds me back. My lungs are on the verge of collapse.

The siren is loud now. It screams in my head. More people crowd me and I shrink away. Nowhere is safe. I know that now. Black stars haze my eyes, so I close them. Close the world out and repeat my mantra. *I am loved. I am supported. I will not be left alone. I am loved. I am supported. I will not be left alone.*

16

I can't be left alone.

OLD HOUSE

I didn't get to go home again until the day after the incident. Marigold was shaking as she led me through the door. The TV was paused at the beginning of a movie. My birthday cake was uncut in the kitchen. A helium balloon boasting the number seventeen was beginning to deflate in the corner of the lounge. The house was silent, but I could still hear the sirens in my ears.

Rita never came home with us.

I took one look at it all and had to run to the bathroom and throw up.

When I could finally stand again, I stumbled to the sink to wash my hands. Rita's dark lipsticks and eyelash curlers and flannel were bunched behind the hot tap, her worn toothbrush balanced atop the rest of her things. Behind my eyes, I saw her lying on the street again and bent back over the toilet, sobbing as a sad trickle of vomit streamed from my lips.

The day of the funeral was a nightmare. Aunt Wilda, Rita's sister, showed up to drive us to the church, and found me sobbing in the hallway, Mari flickering between sympathy and frustration, Rowena shouting at me and Honey trying to mediate the situation. By the time Aunt Wilda got us all in the car, we were already late. We made quite an entrance to the church, the five of us in various states of disorder as we burst into the room. Dishevelled hair, tear stained faces, crumpled clothes – we had all embodied grief.

A lot of people turned up. Rita's co-workers. Her old band members. Extended family. Mari's book club members. The kids Rita coached football to every Saturday. We sat at the front of the church in the pew reserved for family, but I could barely look up from my lap. I knew that several metres away, Rita lay in a black coffin, still and stiff. When Mari nudged me and asked if I wanted to say anything, I felt like my tongue was slick with tar and I choked on all the words I wanted to say. I choked on my goodbyes. We skipped the wake at Rita's favourite pub and headed home. That's when Mari told us to pack our bags. She told us she'd talked it all over with Aunt Wilda. We'll be staying with her until things level out.

But I don't want to go.

It's moving day. I haven't packed, which is why Honey is rushing around my room, still managing to pack neatly in a hurry. I should help her. But part of me is convinced we're not actually going to go.

"Do you want anything handy for the journey? I've not packed your iPod or your book of fairy tales so you can have those in the car," Honey says. I just shrug, staring at my hands. I can tell she wants to say something, but after a few moments, she carries on packing. I wish time would slow down, but it only seems to speed up as Honey secures the final cardboard box with masking tape. When I look up, the room is stripped bare. I took my time making myself at home here – I never had that many possessions when I was in care, but since I moved here, it's amazing how much I've accumulated. All my posters and photographs have been taken off the walls, my stationery and notepads boxed away, my books taking up an entire box by themselves. Honey stands in the centre of the room, awkward now that she doesn't have anything to keep her hands busy. She twirls her hair around her finger.

"Should I...should I take the boxes outside? Aunt Wilda should be here soon."

I don't reply. Honey chews the ends of her hair. She tries to catch my eye, but I look away so I don't have to face her. She sighs, shuffling towards the door. She waits a few moments before picking up a box and leaving. I sigh, sinking back onto my bed. I feel terrible. As awful as this is for Rowena and I, it's ten times more painful for her. She was Rita's only biological child. I should be comforting her the way Honey's tried to comfort me. But even looking at her right now is hard.

She just looks so much like her.

I should find Mari. We've not talked much in the days since the accident. She's mostly been shut away in her room, talking to Aunt Wilda on the phone. I head across the landing, passing Rowena's room where she's lying on her stripped down bed, her headphones clamped over her ears. Downstairs, I can hear Honey keeping herself busy, shifting boxes outside. Marigold's room is at the end of the corridor, but I can't see if she's inside. The door is only slightly ajar, no light coming from inside. But there's music playing quietly. A song by Rita's old band. I knock on the door and receive no answer, so I head in anyway.

Mari's lying on the bed, her face buried in Rita's favourite sweater. Her shoulders are shaking, and at first I think she's crying. But then I realise she's laughing. She looks up at me as I enter, her eyes glistening with tears, but the corners of her lips curved upwards. She pats the bed beside her.

"Come here, Lori. I'm reminiscing."

I shuffle over to sit beside Mari. She's returned to smelling Rita's sweater, her eyes closed.

"I was just remembering the first time you came to stay with us. When we were still fostering. You and Rita were so nervous. Rita was worried that you wouldn't like her, and the whole time we were at dinner, she didn't know how to talk to you. It was the first time I saw her afraid of anything. You know how she always was, nothing much fazed her. I had to be the one to tell her to stop being ridiculous and get on with it, which just seems so funny to me now. I left to go to the bathroom and when I came back the pair of you were huddled by her old tape deck, listening to her band. And that night when you went to sleep, she said you were perfect. She loved you from the very first day."

The story makes my stomach twist. I never knew she felt that way. Rita was never an emotive person – she kept herself to herself, always strictly business. She was caring, but always in a detached kind of way. I can't remember a time where she ever seemed nervous, or scared. She was the opposite to me in that sense. I wish she told me that story herself. There's so much I wish she'd said now. So much I wish I had said too.

"Mari?"

"Mmm?"

"I don't want to leave."

Mari sighs. She's never been very good at hiding her frustrations with me, or anyone to be honest. She's a much more open book than Rita ever was. She wipes her eyes as she sits up. She stares around her. Unlike me, Mari's leaving a lot behind. Mostly Rita's things. The room screams of her. The Beatles posters on the wall. The pile of ripped jeans and big sweaters on top of an old chair, waiting to be put away. A hairbrush stranded on the dresser, hundreds of her curly blonde hairs trapped in the bristles. Marigold reaches into her pocket and finds a handful of Rita's metal rings. They clink together in her palm. She slides them on to her fingers, but they look wrong on her bony hands.

"I can't stay here," Marigold says eventually. "She's too...present."

"Isn't that a good thing?"

Marigold sighs again, but this time it's harder to hear. The pain on her face tells me she's desperate to cry, but she won't. She's too stubborn. She tilts her hand and the rings slide easily from her fingers onto the bed.

"No. It's not. I can't live in my past. The way you couldn't live in yours. And you came here to escape that. Do you understand?"

I do. Here in this room, it's easy to pretend she's still alive. Everything is where she left it. Staying here would be like living in a house where there's been an earthquake. Where everything looks normal, but the tremors have made everything shift an inch to the left, and everything isn't quite as it should be.

I shut the door behind me as I leave Rita's room. I know I won't go back there again. My hand finds the bannister on the landing and I use it to keep me steady as I walk. I'm taking in everything about the house. I want to remember it. Mari's right. This may have been my house for a while, but it was Rita's home. The place where she belonged. It can never be the same place without her here. I was starting to think I belonged there too. But things will be different now.

I guess my birthday wish didn't come true.

I hear the screech of tires outside and jump. I have to remind myself that it's just Aunt Wilda arriving, not a replay of the nightmarish evening of my birthday. It takes me a minute to calm myself, digging out a sour candy from my pocket. I've been getting through so many these past few weeks that my teeth are starting to hurt. I take one last look at my empty bedroom and then head downstairs to greet my aunt.

Honey rushes outside and embraces Wilda on the driveway. Honey and Aunt Wilda look even more alike than Honey and Rita – they have the same slim frame, spidery arms and long legs. Rita was shorter, broader, curvier. But Wilda's unruly hair is so much like Rita's that it hurts. When Wilda looks up and sees me, I have to swallow back tears. She meets me on the doorstep, enveloping me in a hug.

"You poor thing. How are you doing?"

I don't reply. I know if I open my mouth, I'll cry. Wilda seems to understand, and she cups my cheeks.

"Let's get you out of here. This is a time for family to be together. We'll have you settled by this evening. Where's your mother?"

I gesture towards the stairs and Wilda leaves me with a squeeze of my hand. Honey has already busied herself with loading Wilda's Jeep, stacking the boxes with neat precision in the trunk.

I hear the clomp of boots on the stairs and know that Rowena has made an appearance. She joins me on the doorstep and we both watch Honey packing. Ro keeps making little huffing noises under her breath, and I know she's desperate to say something - she's just waiting for me to bite.

"What's up?" I ask her. She huffs again, but she's clearly glad I took her not so subtle hint.

"I hate that Mari's making us move," she mutters. "We were finally getting settled for once. Now she's digging up the roots again."

I nod. Ro was finally making friends at school, finding a crowd that she fit in with. She's not the easiest person to get along with – it doesn't help that she looks a little scary. Her hair is sliced into a black bob with a fringe as severe as her expression, and she tends to carry a 'don't-mess-with-me' vibe. I'm not scared of her – I've known her long enough to know that she's harmless. But to an outsider approaching her, she might as well have a *Keep Out* sign stuck to her forehead.

"You'll make new friends," I promise. Rowena rolls her eyes, but her heart isn't in it. Her gaze drops to the floor, and she leans against the doorframe.

"Rita wouldn't have made us move," she says quietly. She's not wrong.

"You want to come say goodbye to the house with me?" I ask her. She looks at me like I just suggested that we set fire to our hair. I take that as my answer and head for the kitchen.

It's strange to see the kitchen so empty. Rita loved cooking and having family dinners at the table. We had birthdays and Christmases and first meetings in this kitchen. We baked cookies and bread and birthday cakes here. I run my fingers over the shiny grey surfaces. Rita's hands were here. They kneaded dough on this counter. If I close my eyes, I can smell the baking, hear the sound of chairs scraping and Rita banging a metal spoon on a pan, announcing that dinner is ready. It's like she's left a handprint on the room, marking it as her's.

The living room smells of lavender. Rita used to light lavender incense for me. She read up on aromatherapy and found that it's meant to have relaxing properties. The smell used to cling to her skin until it was like she emitted the smell herself. That was when she decided that the colours of the room should match, and she painted the walls lilac overnight to surprise us. If you look closely, there are drips of paint on the carpet all around the room because she forgot to lay down newspaper for the task.

The bathroom still has her things sprawled across the sink. Her bath salts are lined on the windowsill by the bath. I bring them to my nose to smell them. They smell like Parma violets and roses. I consider taking one for myself, but I don't want to disturb what Rita left behind. I put everything back where I found it.

The house is like a museum dedicated to her memory. Everywhere I look, I see family photographs hanging from the walls. Every square inch of this place seems to trigger some kind of memory. As I head for the stairs, I can recall the first time I made Rita laugh out loud as she stood at the top, gripping the bannister as she wheezed. I remember walking by once in the middle of the night to find Rita and Rowena sitting together on the bottom step, talking softly. Every step in between reminds me of the times Rita chased Marigold up the stairs, the pair of them cackling as though they were teenagers. I feel winded by it all. How am I supposed to leave it behind?

When I return to the front of the house, Rowena is outside helping Honey with the boxes. I can hear Wilda and Mari talking upstairs in soft voices. I slip into the porch and stare at our shoe rack. Rita's Timberland boots are the only ones left on the wooden shelf. I pick them up, running the worn shoelaces through my fingers. I hold them for a long time, the yellow leather coarse, but soft and worn. Like Rita.

I feel hands on my shoulders. Skeletal fingers dig into my skin and I close my eyes.

"You can have those if you want," Mari says gently. I nod, putting the shoes on the ground and slipping my feet into them. They're snug and warm and somehow, I feel a little better already. Like every step I take will bring Rita with me.

"Are you ready, hun?" Wilda asks, offering her hand. Wilda isn't much more than a stranger to me, but I take it, taking a deep breath. I have to learn to trust this woman who is giving us our new life.

"I guess so."

Mari takes my other arm as we step out of the house. She closes the door gently behind her, as though not to disturb someone inside. She smiles at me, tears in her eyes.

"Don't worry, Lori. It'll all be okay. When one door closes, another opens."

NEW HOUSE

This isn't going to be home. I think we can all tell that straight away. Honey peers out of the window, analysing the street with a critical eye. Every house we've passed on this road looks exactly the same, with neat gardens out front beside weedless driveways and shiny silver cars. It's not a posh area, but you can tell the people here pride themselves on their immaculate neighbourhood. I can see now why Rita never wanted to visit her sister here. The world here is so bland that it's hard to believe that the houses are filled with all sorts of people, not just clones. I once craved this kind of ordinary life after my upbringing, but Rita showed us a world of technicolor. There's no coming back front hat.

"It's very...nice," Mari comments. Rowena snorts, glaring out the window. She's already written it off as the last place on earth she wants to be. Wilda rounds a corner and tries to catch our eyes in the rear-view mirror.

"Home sweet home, girls."

I peer out the window as the car curves into a driveway. Like the other houses on the street it's neat as a pin, with a slanted roof and two windows protruding out of it. There's a little patch of grass out at the front, and a driveway just big enough for Wilda's car. Honey chews her lip, sinking back into her seat. The car comes to a stop and we all sit in silence. It's almost as though if we don't move, or say anything, then this won't be real.

"Should we...would you like to go inside?" Wilda asks, breaking the spell. Mari sniffs and reluctantly opens the passenger door, hopping down from the car. Honey follows suit, Rowena shuffling out of the middle seat to get to the door. But I stay put. I stroke the book of fairy tales resting on my lap. It feels familiar, unlike everything else here. The house is unfamiliar. Aunt Wilda is unfamiliar, to an extent. Even being in a car is unfamiliar – neither Rita or Mari ever drove. It smells like pine and de-icer. But it's less daunting staying here than committing myself to a new house, a new life I didn't ask for. Wilda knocks on my window and I snap out of my daze, hugging my book to my chest.

"Lori, darling...come inside, I'll make you some tea."

I don't drink tea. Anyone who knows me would know that. Suddenly, I'm terrified. I'm going to be living with a stranger. This is all too much. I scramble away from the door, trapped. Wilda clearly doesn't know how to respond and disappears for a moment. A few seconds later, Honey's face appears in the window, her eyes soft.

"Lori, come on! It's lovely inside. You can have the first pick of the beds if you come in now..."

I know it's a ploy to get me out of the car, but I feel safer with Honey than I do with Wilda. I feel guilty, knowing that Wilda has opened up her home to us, but she still feels too distant from me to trust her. When Honey opens the car door and I clamber out, she takes my hand to guide me up the front path and to the house.

It's easy to see how different Wilda is to Rita just from her house. I've met her before, of course, but only at our house, in Rita's territory. She was always awkward around Rita. Whenever she visited, she remained perched on the edge of the settee like she was scared to touch anything. Here, where Wilda is at home, she seems like she fits perfectly in the jigsaw of the street. She may share the same genes as Rita, but they're nothing alike. This whole place looks like it's been doused in bleach to keep it clean. Rita used to joke that Wilda kept a bottle of Febreeze in her bag at all times 'in case of emergencies.'

I step through the porch and into the front room. The walls are decorated with gold and blue wallpaper, and the carpet is cream. We could never have had cream carpet back home – Rita would spill something on it within moments of it being laid. There's only one sofa, but it's huge – it's one of those ones that has a corner, and a footstool to match the leaf patterned cushions. It's duck egg blue to match the walls, and the whole room seems bright and airy. It's surprising, and it's nice. Somehow, it's a relief from the clutter back home. I feel like a traitor for even thinking such a thing.

I stand awkward in the room, trying to keep my breathing steady. Do I sit down? Do I compliment the room? Do I ask for a tour or just make myself comfortable? A thousand thoughts fight for attention in my head. Wilda sweeps in from the kitchen and smiles at me.

"Why don't I get you some dinner ready while you go and take a look at your rooms? It's been a long day."

I'm grateful for the distraction, though it's clear Wilda noticed my discomfort. Honey, who still hasn't let go of my arm, drags me through the kitchen and veers left in the hallway to go upstairs. The landing is dark, but the rooms on either side of the stairway are as bright as the living room. Both have double beds so I can only assume they're Wilda and Mari's rooms. We continue across the landing. There's a box room to the left which Rowena has already made herself at home in. She was desperate for privacy, so Honey and I agreed to share the other room. I wasn't particularly keen to have my own room anyway. It would only make me feel more alone.

The bedroom is nice. It's hard to find a descriptor that describes it better. The walls are pastel pink, and there are white curtains with a rose print draped from the large window that looks out onto the street. There are twin beds with duvets to match the curtains, and white bookcases big enough to house both mine and Honey's books. In the corner, there's an alcove that I can imagine sitting in to read. There's a desk that I'm certain Honey will hog and cover in all of her study notes. I grasp for a more positive word than nice to describe my environment. Maybe it'll feel a little homelier when we move our things in here. I've only ever called one place home, and we just left it behind. This will just take getting used to. At least here, away from the eyes of the rest of my family, I can try to relax.

I flop down on the bed furthest from the door, smushing my face into the pillow. Now that I'm inside, I feel like an idiot for making a scene in the car. Being in this new place has made me nervous. More than usual.

Mari and Honey are used to it by now, and Rowena has known me long enough to be willing to put up with it, but Wilda barely knows me. We've met a handful of times, but her priority was always seeing Honey and Rita, not me. Her blood relatives. I would sit quietly during her visits and try to camouflage into the sofa. She's never seen me break down before today. All I can think is how stupid Wilda must think I am.

"She doesn't think you're stupid."

I didn't realise I was even voicing my thoughts. Honey is watching me, wide eyed, sat cross legged on her bed. She runs a hand over the silky material of her pillow. "Aunt Wilda has made a lot of effort to make us feel at home, hasn't she? I think she's very welcoming. She was very chatty in the car."

"Yes she was."

"You don't need to be scared of her. She's family."

I nod, but I don't mention that sometimes families don't live up to normal expectations. Not that Honey would ever know that. I've often heard people say that you can't hate your parents – even if you don't always get along, you love them unconditionally, because they're family. Girls like Honey can say that with ease. I can't, so much. So as much as I want to trust Aunt Wilda and her intentions, I can't do it so easily. For years, she and Rita were little more than acquaintances, only seeming to meet up out of duty rather than love. That's enough to put me on edge. If Rita wasn't close with Wilda, then I'm guessing there was a reason for it.

I roll off my bed and stand to look out of the window. Outside, everything is quiet. There's no one out on the street. No kids playing, or cars driving by. Honey joins me in looking.

"I like it. It's pretty."

I can only nod. It is pretty, in a uniform, perfect kind of way. It's just different. Nothing like we're used to. I've never been in a neighbourhood like this, let alone lived in one. Before I found a home with Rita and Marigold, I lived all over; children's homes stuck in forgotten corners of rough neighbourhoods, foster homes in industrial towns, cold flats with boarded up windows that smelt of smoke. Here, the colourful, light room seems a little utopian. Too good to be true.

"It'll just take some time to settle in. I suppose tomorrow we've got a lot to do. We'll have to look for local colleges, unpack, check out the buses…"

I haven't thought of all of that. Life since the accident just seems to have come to a complete standstill, like we've paused our story on the TV. I'm not sure I'm ready to hit play again. There are still fresh reminders all around me of what happened. The scabs on my knees where I fell in the street. The dreams every night of what happened. I know I should attempt to move on – Rita would want us to. But I can't imagine going to a strange new college with strange new people and then coming home to this odd new house. The thought makes me feel nauseous.

"Can't it wait a while?"

"Well term's already started...we'll be playing catch up if we leave it any longer. And we've got to start thinking about applying to university in the next few weeks. We'll need to be able to say what college we attend."

I feel sick. I sit down on my bed, suddenly dizzy. Honey frowns.

"Are you okay?"

I fish in my pocket for a sour sweet, but I find the packet empty. I swallow hard.

"I'm just...adjusting."

Honey smiles with sympathy, patting my arm. "I'll give you some space. Maybe I can go and give Aunt Wilda a hand with dinner."

I'm almost glad to see her go. What I need right now is to be alone, and Honey knows as much. I need to figure out how I'll slot myself into this new life. It's not as easy as just unpacking my possessions. It's like I'm going to need to unpack myself too. I need time to accept that this is it – this is how things will be from now on.

I smooth down the sheets on my bed. It feels strange to think that it now belongs to me. It feels weird to know I'll be sharing a room again too – I haven't done that since I left the care system. In fact, everything is strange. I could be living someone else's life right now and it would feel more normal than this. And that's when I remember a way I can escape reality for a while.

It takes me a few minutes to get myself set up. My laptop is still somewhere in the car, but I grab my book of fairy tales and smooth down the first page. The book was a gift from Honey on my last birthday. When she found out that my birth parents never read me fairy tales as a child, she said she knew exactly what she had to buy me. Honey has impeccable taste, of course – the land of fairy stories is the place of my dreams. Rowena thinks it's childish, but she thinks everything about my attitude is. I don't care. I love to flick through the pages. Even when I don't read the stories, I look at the accompanying artwork, or imagine what happily ever after actually means. It feels like home.

Books like this make me wish I was an artist. The worlds painted in the book are so detailed they seem real, but better than reality, with their vivid green and teal and lilac images spilling across the pages. I flick to

the final story in the book, and my favourite –
Cinderella. There's a picture of her in a sky-blue dress,
one crystal-slippered foot pointed in front of her.

It took me a while to realise why I love Cinderella so
much. I think it's because she manages to make the best
of a bad situation. She's a slave to her family, but she
never complains, and she works hard. She's confident
and stands up for herself when her sisters and step
mother push her down. And then she's kind – pure at
heart, and untainted by her terrible life.

I flick through the pages to look at the pictures – it's
just as good as reading the story. There's a picture of the
fairy godmother transforming Cinderella, floating
gracefully above her with her wand poised. Cinderella is
twirling in the picture, her rags falling away to reveal her
ball gown. I smile to myself, tracing the picture. That's
the other thing that I love about the story. Cinderella
always has someone protecting her. Someone who cares
when no one else seems to. I feel a pang in my heart, a
tear stinging my eye.

The fairy godmother reminds me of *her*.

Aunt Wilda's voice snaps me out of the story. She's
calling me to dinner, back to the real world. I sigh and
close the book. I guess we can't always have a fairy
godmother to rescue us.

PATIO

Wilda has gone all out for our first night in the house. I expected when I came down the stairs to be ushered into the dining room, but Wilda has other plans. I find her in the kitchen, bent over the stove. Her hair has frizzed over the heat of the pan she's attacking with a wooden spoon. She abandons her post for a minute to guide me towards the back door, a hand on my back.

"I thought since it's a nice night, we could sit out on the patio," she says. "I think you'll like my little fairy grove."

Outside, it's getting dark, but the garden is glowing with fairy lights. They're draped on the shrubbery and above the bottom floor windows. They're even wound up the umbrella that sits in the centre of the patio table. The table has four black garden chairs around it, plus an old deckchair which looks out of place in the pristine garden. The table sits snug in the corner between the garden wall and the fence that separates Wilda's garden from next door. The flowers in the garden wall are drooping a little, folding themselves away for winter. Wilda's right – the garden is pretty special.

Rowena is a little less impressed. As she follows Wilda and I out of the house, she folds her arms, raising an eyebrow.

"Cute," she says dryly. "The kitchen smells like burning. I thought you should know."

"Oh gosh," Wilda says, running back inside to tend to the unfolding kitchen disaster. Rowena rolls her eyes.

"*Oh gosh*? Who talks like that? Just say the F word and be done with it."

"Was that necessary?"

"What? I was just saying."

"With a heavy attitude."

Rowena scowls, but lowers her head in shame. She kicks at a lone weed growing between the cobbles. "I guess she'll get used to it."

I raise an eyebrow. Rowena shoots to kill every time she opens her mouth to speak. We've all felt the devastating blow of her words. And she's right, we've got used to it. But it doesn't make it right, and Wilda deserves it less than anyone.

"You're being rude."

Rowena's head snaps up again, her brows scrunched. "Well I didn't ask to be here."

Before I can lecture her further, Honey and Mari join us on the patio. We all stand awkwardly by the door, waiting to be invited to sit down. Somehow, it feels rude to just make ourselves at home, even if this is where we live for now. Wilda returns, her hair seemingly even frizzier than two minutes ago.

"Disaster averted," she says, grinning. "Sit yourselves down! Dinner will be out in just a tiff."

Rowena smirks and I know she's thinking about the word tiff. Not the sort of language we're used to – especially considering that Rita often swore like a sailor. But Honey doesn't bat an eye. In many ways, she's more like Wilda than she was ever like Rita.

Wilda returns with a plate of burgers and a bowl of pasta. Salad, buns and chips follow.

"I know kids go mad for this stuff," Wilda says as she finally sinks into the old deckchair. Her head hovers just above the table, like she's a child peering over a shop counter. "I've got to admit, I've never cooked burgers before. I hope they're alright."

"They look fine," Mari says with a tight smile. Rowena snatches up the salad servers and dumps half the bowl on her plate. Wilda blinks at her. Her mouth opens, but shuts after a moment. She turns to me and smiles.

"Would you like a burger, dear?"

I can't stand burgers, but I don't want to look rude so I take one, hoping the ketchup and salad will mask the texture that always makes me cringe. Mari nods to me with a small smile, grateful. Honey constructs her burger with care and Mari subtly scoops some pasta onto Rowena's plate.

"Well isn't it nice to have the family together?" Wilda says. Everyone stares at her, and she blushes, realising her mistake. I know she didn't mean anything by it, but it's turned Rowena's expression even more sour. She clears her throat, busying herself with piling food onto her plate.

"So..." Wilda says, searching for a suitable topic. "Did you girls look at colleges yet? I know you've been busy, but I just wondered..."

Honey sits up straight. She's in her element now. "I have. Greenbank looks really great."

"Greenbank, huh? Aiming high, I see!"

"I suppose. But both Lori and I have the grades to attend. I've looked at the curriculum too, and there's a very wide choice."

"I've had a nosy myself. It does look like an excellent institution."

"Honey, we talked about this remember?" Mari says. She's not eaten anything so far. "The bus pass costs far too much."

"Oh, Marigold! I can cover it!" Wilda says with a dismissive wave of her hand. "We want the best for the girls, don't we? Greenbank College get excellent results. Even if Honey will only be attending for her last year, it'll look great on her personal statement."

"We can't ask that of you. You've done so much already," Mari says, her lips tight. Honey blushes, and I know she feels bad for putting Mari in this position. She hates taking charity as it is.

"I want to do this for the girls. I want them to have the best possible start in life," Wilda says, wiping a blob of ketchup from her lips with her pinkie finger. "But we shan't have money talk at the table. Will you be keeping your same subjects, Honey? Still headed for med school I hope?"

"I think so. I wrote my personal statement over the summer."

"Aren't you a doll! So well prepared. How about you, Lori? What have you picked to do?"

I'm surprised at the sudden attention I'm receiving. I try to chew faster to finish my mouthful while Wilda watches, smiling patiently.

"Umm. Well. Honey told me that Greenbank offers a Creative Writing class. And then English, I guess. And Mari thinks I should do what I picked originally, which was Psychology and History."

"Well isn't that an interesting mix! I think you'll fit in just great at Greenbank, Lori. Marigold tells me you're a little nervous about going to college, but the students there are very conscientious and hard working. One of my co-workers had a son who went through that school, and he left with excellent grades," Wilda tells me. I stare at my plate, nervous to meet her enthusiastic gaze. I can't believe Mari told her I'm nervous.

"Of course, Rowena's a little young to be thinking about all that! It'll be GCSE's first!" Wilda tries to catch Rowena's eye, but she's busy stabbing at pieces of lettuce. "Have you any ideas of what you'd like to do in the future?"

Rowena says nothing, her eyebrows knitted into a scowl.

"Rowena," Mari pushes. "Your aunt is trying to talk to you."

Ro finally glares in Wilda's direction. "I'm thirteen. I'm too young to be thinking about GCSEs."

"Right! Right, of course," Wilda says, flustered. She tucks her frizzy hair behind her reddened ears. She struggles for something to say, staring at Rowena's plate. "Well, it'll be so nice to have you enrolled at my school! I promise I won't embarrass you in the corridors or anything, though. Don't you want a burger, dear?"

Rowena snorts. "Yeah. Because vegetarians eat burgers."

Wilda's whole body seems to be blushing now. Her neck, her nose and ears are all scarlet. "Oh, I'm sorry! I had no idea. I would have bought some veggie burgers if I'd known. You must be starving! How about some more pasta, then?"

Rowena looks at Wilda like she just smacked her across the face. "Do you even know what's in that stuff? Have you ever *heard* of carbs?"

"Rowena!"

"No, no, it's okay!" Wilda assures, flapping her arms around as though trying to break up a fight. Maybe she thinks Rowena is about to stand up and hit someone. In her haste, she knocks over her glass of juice, spilling it over the plate of burgers. She looks close to tears, trying to salvage some of the food by shuffling the plates and all the while trying not to cause more chaos.

"I'll just...get some paper towels," she says. She half walks, half runs into the house. Rowena lets her fork clatter on her plate, leaning back and folding her arms.

"Well, this is going well."

"Rowena," Honey hisses. It's not often she loses her temper, but she doesn't look happy.

"She acts like she farts money. 'Oh sure, I'll fork out a grand for the bus, no problem.' Who does she think she is?"

"That's your aunt you're talking about. Don't be such a cheeky little brat," Marigold says, slapping her napkin down onto her lap. "What did I ask of you, Rowena? Did I or did I not ask you to behave? Couldn't you do that for just one night, instead of making my life so bloody hard?"

I hear Honey gasp. My throat feels tight. I've never heard Mari talk this way before. I guess there's a reason that she always let Rita handle our discipline. She's always had a temper of her own. Rowena is red in the face, glaring at Mari.

"Doesn't it bother you? The way we've barely heard a peep from her in years, and now she's swanning around, throwing money at us, playing like everything is *just swell* and *tickety boo*? You say I have no respect? Her sister's been dead for five minutes and she's already dancing on her grave."

"Don't be ridiculous."

"She's trying to make up for lost time by paying us off. She feels guilty because Rita is dead and she's here, alone, swimming in cash and living a cushy life. Well, I never asked to be here."

"Is there somewhere you'd rather be?" Mari asks. Rowena smirks, scraping her chair as she stands.

"I would rather be back with my real Mum, if that's what you're insinuating. At least she left me the hell alone."

Marigold stands, giving Rowena a warning look. "Don't you dare storm off. And you're grounded."

"Oh no. Stuck in the house when I've got no friends to go and visit and no better place to be than my bedroom. Boo hoo."

Rowena stomps her way back into the house. Wilda is standing in the doorway, a paper towel in her hand. She's not smiling anymore, her mouth slightly agape. Rowena pushes past her and even from outside, I can hear her boots connecting like a punch on every step on the stairs. I chew my nail, sinking down further into my chair. Honey's eyes are watering and Mari stares into space, her face unreadable.

I can't bear the awkwardness. I stand up, taking my plate with me. My food is mostly untouched. As I pass Wilda in the doorway, I want to say something, but all that comes out is "thanks for dinner." She regards me with a nod, but she's given up. Maybe Ro was right, in a way. She's been playing Happy Families all evening, but she may as well be some long-lost cousin that none of us have heard of.

We're living in a house together, but none of us know her at all.

COLLEGE

"You ready to go, Lori?"

I stand stiff in the hallway. I got up two hours early to prepare for today. I laid out an outfit last night to wear, but now, my battered jeans and casual t-shirt seem like I've made no effort. Or maybe I look like I'm trying too hard to look like I'm not trying. The thought makes me cringe. I consider changing into the jumper I tried on, or the dress and boots that Honey calls quirky. But I know no matter what I wear, I won't feel prepared for this day.

"The bus will be here in a minute…" Honey says, shifting from foot to foot. "I don't want to push you, but I can't miss my first day."

"I know, I'm sorry. I know this is important to you," I say. I take a deep breath. I can feel my breakfast churning in my stomach. But Honey takes my arm and I know it's time to go.

Marigold appears from the living room. She's still in her dressing gown, and she droops over her coffee. She tries for a smile as she examines me and Honey, and leans to kiss each of our cheeks.

"Study hard," she says, her voice flat.

"We will."

"Come on," Honey says softly. I let her lead me out the door before I change my mind.

I'm glad we don't have to cross the road to get to the bus stop. It's just a few paces from Wilda's house, and it's empty save for us. Honey taps her foot, impatient.

"What if the bus is late? Wilda already left for work, and she doesn't have time to drive us there anyway. It looks bad if we're late on our first day. "

It's moments like this when I realise Honey and I really are alike. She's just as anxious as me, when it comes down to it. We just have different ideas of what disaster looks like to us.

"It'll be here. It can't just not show up," I promise her, though I'm wishing that it wouldn't.

Honey lets out a long puff of air, her fingers twitching. "If I show up late, what are they going to think? This college is super prestigious. You don't just get in with any old grades."

"I know, Honey. But it's not your fault if the bus is late, is it?"

"Right. You're right. Think logically."

That's the difference between me and her. She knows how to keep her nerves reigned in. She tells herself that things will be alright, and she believes it. I don't know how she does it. I watch her take a deep breath, moving her hands to her long hair. She fiddles with it, weaving it into a neat plait. When the bus arrives five minutes later, half the left side of her head is plaited.

I know what college buses are like – crowded and stale smelling and full of boys cramped on the backseat, shouting comments at everyone who dares step onto the bus. But we're at one of the first stops, and when the bus arrives, Honey picks out the perfect seat for us, right at the front behind the driver. If I sit by the window, I'm mostly out of sight. She knows me well.

The bus starts to move and I take my timetable out of my bag, scanning it. I have a free period first thing. I'm not sure if it's a good or bad thing – it'll give me some time to hide out in the library, but I would rather dive straight in with a lesson so I don't have the time to overthink it. Still, maybe I can distract myself by exploring the books. No one scary hangs out in a library. It's a well-known fact in a nerd's world.

Honey leans to look at my timetable and I get a glimpse of hers. My eyes widen. Her timetable is completely full with no free periods.

"Is there a mistake with the timetable? You'll have to go to the office and get it sorted out," I tell her, but she shakes her head, blushing.

"I decided to take on two extra subjects. To set me apart from the crowd when I'm applying to university.."

"I didn't even know you could do that,'" I say, taking up the timetable to get a better look. "Physics, Biology, Chemistry, Maths *and* Further Maths. Are you crazy?"

"No," Honey says indignantly, snatching the sheet back. "Further Maths is just building on the knowledge I already have, and maths is so easy it might as well be an after-school club. If it becomes too much, they told me on the phone that I can drop them. But I'm sure I can handle it."

Knowing her, she can. Why she'd want to, I'm not sure.

"You know med school will want you without all this stuff, right?"

Honey shrugs, taking out a maths textbook. She opens a page and begins doodling the answers to an equation on the side of the page. "Just to be sure."

"Well, why not just do one or the other? You're already doing an extra A Level. Most people only do three-"

"Just leave it, please, Lori. I'm already nervous enough."

You're not the only one I think as we pull up at the next stop. I stare out of the window, watching the next group of people get on board. Sure enough, a huge group of boys board here, pushing and shoving each other as they head for the back seat. Then, in the corner of my eye, I see a blue blur as someone runs by. They miss the door by a few inches and have to backtrack several steps to get to the bus.

I see the bus driver shake his head as the girl boards. She's out of breath, but she's grinning. I can't help, but stare at her. The girl is short and curvy with a sweet round face free of makeup. A pair of glasses sit slightly askew on her face and she fixes them with a slight nudge of her finger. Her short blonde hair levels with her chin, chic and cool in a way I've always wished my hair would fall.

This girl is simply gorgeous.

"Thanks, Bernie. You keep me in shape," she says.

"Try getting up five minutes earlier. You might actually make it to your stop on time and you won't have to run."

"Ah, but where's the fun in that?" she asks. I find myself smiling. I look to Honey to see if she saw what happened, but she's focused on her textbook. When I look up, the bus is moving, and the girl is wobbling down the aisle, her hands fumbling for each yellow handlebar to keep her steady. I take her in once again. She's wearing a blue faux leather jacket with multicoloured leopard print on it. It should be the ugliest garment in the world, but it looks so good on her that I forget how garish it is. I blush and look away from her. The last thing I need is for a cute girl to see me staring at her.

She slips into the seat behind us and for some reason, my heart freezes. I hear her earphones clanking as she untangles them. Moments later, I hear tinny music coming from the headphones. She hums along as though she's alone in her room, not on a crowded bus.

She distracts me the whole way to college, humming the entire journey. Sometimes she gasps when a new song comes on, excited by the prospect of it. There's something relaxing about her humming. It's not particularly tuneful, but it's warm and thick like honey. I find myself wanting to hum along, but I can't imagine how Honey would react. Humming along with strangers isn't exactly normal.

It's only when the college appears before us that I begin to feel my nerves returning. I've been so enchanted by the girl behind us that I forgot to be scared. Honey grabs my hand, her thin hands clamping over my clumpy fingers. Her hands are steady, but I can feel mine shaking between hers. Hers are cool and mine are clammy with sweat. Not for the first time, I wish I was her.

The bus stops and people push and shove to get off. Honey waits, her hands still on mine. I watch everyone leave, including the girl sitting behind me. I watch her sashay off the bus. She yells to a boy standing in front of the college, and throws herself into his open arms. For some reason, I have to look away.

"Time to go," Honey tells me. I swallow, closing my eyes. If I concentrate hard enough, her hand feels like Rita's. If she were here, she'd tell me I can do this. She'd believe in me. That's what I have to focus on.

"Okay," I say. I pick up my bag and clutch it to my chest. Marigold insisted I should have a backpack for college, but I'm always too nervous to have it on my back in case someone steals from it. The perks of constant anxiety. Honey frowns, but says nothing as we get off the bus, thanking the driver. We're barely off the bus when he closes the doors and drives away.

No going back now.

Honey stares up at the building. It's a mismatched set of blocks, like it was built by a young child playing with Lego. The front entrance is surrounded by students. You can tell apart the first years and the seconds – the first years are squeaky clean with brand new rucksacks not so different to mine, and they're all wearing their best clothes. The second years like Honey seem to have made less effort in their sweats and scuffed trainers. Their rucksacks are torn at the sides, binder folders peeping through the rips. Honey smiles, taking a deep breath.

"Do you want to go in together?"

I shake my head. I know Honey wants to get to her first class early. I think she thinks that if she stands around outside, she might be able to talk to someone about quantum mechanics or something. Who knows. Maybe she can here.

"It's okay. I'm going to the library."

"Will you find it okay? Do you want me to walk you there?"

The question irritates me a little. Why she thinks she'd have a better idea where the library is, I'm not sure. After all, neither of us have been here before. It sometimes feels like she thinks I'm incapable of anything, just because I get anxious. But I don't say anything because I know deep down that she has reason to doubt me, and she's only trying to help. I just shake my head. Honey tightens her bag straps, grinning. I give her a weak smile.

"Feeling at home?"

She nods. "More than I have in weeks."

Rita hangs between us, an unspoken presence. Honey looks up, as though that's where she is. I know she's thinking of her. Wondering what she'd make of our new life without her. Honey sighs, looking a little less pleased. But her face is still set in determination.

"Right. I'm going in. You'll be alright?"

Probably not. "Of course."

"Text me if you need me."

I nod, but I won't. I won't drag her from her studies to baby me. I have some pride. I wave to her as she bounds into the building, her ponytail and backpack bobbing, and I know that I'm on my own.

I miss a breath and it makes my chest tighten, but I force myself to move into the building. Inside smells like sweat and food. To my left, the cafeteria is buzzing with people. Right near the door, a large group of boys gather around a table, over-spilling from the benches and leaning on the bars that separate them from their table and the stairs. They all wear shades of grey and black, caps pulled far over their eyes. I decide right away that no matter what, I'm not walking through the cafeteria.

I rush through to the corridors, looking for a way out. I veer off into a toilet to calm myself for a few moments and to splash my face with water. I leave the bathroom with my face dripping, and I swear everyone is looking at me. I dip my head, trying not to notice that my heart is struggling to keep up.

I burst outside into a busy courtyard after seeing a sign for the library. Outside, students gather under a shelter, smoking. Teachers that look as young as the students stop to chat with them, smoking cigarettes of their own. I can imagine what Rita would say – all these intelligent people, all thinking it's a good idea to smoke. Where did they find that logic? I can smell the cigarettes. They clog my nose, making breathing a harder task than it already is today. I head quickly for the metal gate on the other side of the courtyard.

I panic when I realise the gate needs a pass. I search my bag frantically, trying to remember where I put mine. It slips out of my bag and I snatch it up, scanning myself through before a queue can form behind me. I half run, half walk to the library, stumbling through the doors into the warmth of the building.

The first thing I notice is the quiet. It's disconcerting for a moment, but then it settles my flailing heart. No one talks in whispers, but there's barely anyone around to hear anyway. I suppose at the start of term, the library isn't the most popular hangout.

I delve deeper into the room. At our old school, the library was being knocked down to make room for a new gym. The school only kept a few books, and most were base texts. But as I look up, I can see there are at least three floors to explore. I'm betting there's more in here than any other school I've attended. I pass the librarian and a few groups of students and make it to the stairs. Then I climb and climb until I reach the top. I open the door and I'm met with an empty room of books.

Perfect.

LIBRARY

Twenty-three minutes have passed. That means thirty until I have to leave here, find my first class and meanwhile, try not to have a panic attack.

Pathetic. It's pathetic really. No wonder most people struggle to have sympathy for me. I probably wouldn't, if I was on the outside, looking in. Why does going to a lesson scare me so much? It's just a classroom. It's just a room filled with people who just want to learn, just want to get by, just like me. That's all I'm being faced with. And yet I'm sitting here, trying to remember how to breathe and thinking of a million ways I can get out of going.

Still, for now I'm alone. I found a comfy corner with a dusty couch that probably hasn't been sat on since last term. It's in a nice spot – the balcony it's on overlooks the rest of the library. But I can't bring myself to read even though I hold a copy of Grimm's tales in my hands. Grimm's tales just aren't the same anyway. I know technically they're where my favourites originated from – Rowena bought me a copy of Grimm's for my birthday as a joke – but they're too chaotic, too cruel. Not something I can find comfort in right now.

"Wow. I think you're the first kid I've seen voluntarily hold a book in ten years."

I look up. A woman is standing, watching me. She's wide hipped and shrouded in a floral top. She has short cropped hair the colour of red wine. Something about her is intimidating, though not conventionally – she's not tall, or muscular, or intimidatingly beautiful. She is frowning, though. I suddenly wonder whether upstairs is restricted access. Teacher's only. But my legs won't move me so I stay sat, looking up at the woman.

"Tablets, mobile phones, laptops...you don't get many kids with their head in a book, even here. Most of the kids you see in here are looking for fact, not fiction - they're only there to trudge through their A Levels and get the hell out."

It seems an odd thing to say – all the girls I've ever known read. Honey reads textbooks for fun. Marigold and Rita used to spend long hours back to back on the sofa, reading fat volumes of Reader's Digest. Even Rowena likes the occasional vampire fic. Of course, I don't say any of this. I simply look at the woman, my heart thudding hard.

The woman sighs into the sofa next to me and I feel myself stiffen. She tips the book in my hand to see the cover.

"It's always the quiet ones. Into all that dark stuff," she says. She sticks a hand to me that's covered in bold metal rings. They remind me of Rita, but I can't be rude and ignore her hand. However, when I stick out my hand to shake hers, she laughs.

"I was hoping for your book, not your hand. Still, at least we're now properly acquainted. Do you have a name?"

I swallow. "Lori."

"Lori...do you happen to be taking a Creative Writing module? There's a Lori that's just been added onto my register. Second period. I'm Mrs Whickam, I lead the English department."

I don't want to say yes, though I know I must. It feels like promising myself to this place. More than being on a register or signing up for classes – now a teacher knows my name, and can put it to a face. I nod reluctantly.

"Excellent. I always like to get to know my students a little. I consider my creative writers a little family. They bring my utmost joy every year. It's good to share creative space, isn't it?"

I'm not entirely sure what she means by that, but I nod. She doesn't stop to see if I agree.

"We've had some real talents come from this course. A lot of the kids in my class go on to study creative writing further. There's a delightful little course in Bangor where you can study it alongside lyricism. I had a girl from my class go there. She's a hit on Youtube. You might have heard of her."

I doubt it, but I smile and hope that constitutes an answer. Mrs Wickham cocks her head to the side.

"And what do you write, Lori? Poetry? Memoir?"

The thought of writing a memoir makes me feel a little sick. My tale feels much too dark to write about. I'm not much of a poet either. I shake my head.

"Well, this wasn't supposed to be a guessing game. Which is it?"

"Prose. Fairy tales," I whisper.

"Explains the book, I suppose. Do you prefer happy fairy stories, or the dark ones?"

"I...the happy ones."

"Did your parents read those to you, as a child?"

I stiffen. My chest tightens. "No. Not that I remember."

"Oh. Well, most girls who are into the whole fairy tale palaver were Disney kids. Not you?"

"No. Not me."

Mrs Wickham watches me for a few moments and I force myself to control my breathing. She frowns and I know she's trying to figure me out. Trying to guess what my problem is. I've found over time that people who like to write also like to create stories about the people around them. She's writing her version of me in her head. I bet she's got me all wrong.

"Well, Lori. I'll see you in second period. And don't look so worried! I don't bite."

I watch her go, my lungs on the verge of failure. As the door shuts, I gasp for air. Her question circles my head. *Did your parents read those to you as a child?* She couldn't have known. She couldn't possibly know how much that question hurt. A reminder of how much my birth parents hurt me. And a fresh reminder that my true parent, Rita, is now gone.

I feel exposed here. The balcony where I sit overlooks the library. Anyone could spot me. I stumble for the bookcases, grappling for their wooden shelves. I run my fingers over the spines of the books and mutter to myself.

"It's fine, everything's fine, she didn't know, she didn't know…"

I half hope Mrs Wickham will come back. Catch me in my manic moment and send me home. But I can't even go home. We live at Wilda's house now. Home isn't home anymore – it's the empty house where we left Rita's ghost to rest. I feel like my family has been scattered far from my reach. I can't run to one member without leaving one behind. I fumble for my phone. My eyes are blurred as I search for Honey's number. But I remember my silent promise to her – that I won't ruin this for her. I have to do this myself. I have to do it alone.

I rest my forehead against the shelf as a shrill bell rings. I check my watch. I only have five minutes until class. Seems time flies when you're having fun. I take a deep breath, wiping my cheeks. They come away black from my mascara, but there's no time to sort out my face. I have a class to get to. There's nothing worse than being late and having everyone stare at you.

The corridors are a blur. Vague outlines of people travel in packs, laughing and talking ringing in my ears. I disassociate from it all. I grip the straps of my bag, trying not to trip over my feet or make a nuisance of myself. My lungs stagger to keep up. I don't really know where I'm going.

"Lori!"

I whip around. Mrs Wickham blurs into view.

"You walked right past the class. Got somewhere better to be?"

It's not meant to sound threatening. I know that. But it does. I scoot past the teacher and scan the classroom. I breathe a sigh of relief. The class is still mostly empty, and the seats at the back of the room have yet to be taken. The best part of college? No seating plan. I head for the back of the room and hope that I might be able to blend in.

I unpack my bag. Pencil-case. Notebook. Phone. Water bottle. I arrange them on my desk. Then I rearrange them in a new order. It takes around a minute. Now, I've got nothing to do but wait.

And then she walks in. My eyes are drawn involuntarily to the door. The girl in the leather jacket, the girl who caught my attention on the bus, is suddenly standing mere metres away. Her jacket is hooked over one of her fingers and slung over her shoulder. I blush as she searches the room for somewhere to sit. Her eyes lock on the desk in front of me and then there she is, pulling out the chair and sitting down. The class is filling fast now, but I concentrate on the girl. She's humming again as she gets herself ready for the class. *Sweet Child of Mine*. My throat closes up. Tears well in my eyes. Rita sang it with her band.

And suddenly Mrs Wickham is closing the door. The class is full. People are looking at me; I'm the new girl. I wasn't here to begin with. I stick out. I focus on my breathing, but it doesn't help. There's no air. No way out. I can hear Mrs Wickham starting to talk. She's saying something about me. I hear my name. But it's like I'm underwater. Unable to see, to hear, to breathe. I'm drowning.

"Lori?" Mrs Wickham's voice is clear for a moment. "Stand up so that everyone can see you. Say something about yourself."

I stand with shaking legs. I force my eyes to focus. Everyone is looking at me. I'm dizzy. I can't breathe.. I grapple for the desk. I miss.

Then I'm falling.

DINING ROOM

I sat in the college office for a long time, trying to control my breathing. The on-site nurse gave me endless cups of water and hinted that I should make my way back to class more than once. Each time, I told her the same thing – I wanted to go home. Eventually, she sighed and rang home. Wilda arrived an hour later and we drove back to her house in silence. She let the windows down a little as she drove, muttering something about me needing air after a fainting spell. But we both know the reason I fainted had nothing to do with being ill. Not physically, at least.

I have a bruise on the side of my face from where I fell, and I've used it to milk my situation for as long as possible. I wake each morning and complain of a headache. Marigold sighs and reluctantly calls college to inform them of my absence. But there's only so many days you can call in sick. Even I know that.

It's always been this way for me. I've always struggled to participate in ordinary life, ever since I was a child.

My past has left me with wounds that don't seem capable of healing, and the anxiety that tears me up in side effects everything I do. Whenever I get sick, I convince myself I'm dying. When I'm forced out of the house, I always consider the worst case scenarios of what might happen while I'm away. Whenever someone says something that seems off to me, I overthink it until I get myself into a rut of terror. I know that's not normal. I know these are problems most people don't have. But as much as I'd like to be an ordinary girl, life never had that intention for me. And now, whenever I think about going back to college, or just stepping foot outside this house, I feel a wave of nausea inside me so strong that I feel like I might actually be sick.

I don't want to do this anymore.

"Will you be going in tomorrow, Lori?" Honey asks. She's perched at the desk with a pile of textbooks that she borrowed from the library. Half of them she brought home for me, and I haven't touched them since. The other half are hers, and there are half a dozen open in front of her. There's no space for her notebook on the table, so she's writing on her knee.

"I don't know," I tell her, but I already know my answer is no. Honey flashes me a smile, but I can tell her heart isn't in it.

"Well, I could email your tutors again? I'm sure they'll understand why you've not turned any work in. You can always pick up the slack when you're...better."

I can't lie to her anymore. I sigh, shuffling to the end of my bed. "Honey, you know that's not why I'm staying home."

She looks at me with feigned innocence. "No?"

"I'm telling them. At dinner."

Honey sighs, turning her back on me. "Your funeral."

I blink in surprise. That's not something she'd usually say. "Are you alright?"

"Fine," she replies instantly, not looking up from her work. I grab my pillow and hug it to my chest. I know Honey's having a hard time settling in at the new college. It's not that she hasn't made new friends – from what I can gather, she's got a whole bunch of people chasing her up, asking her to parties and wanting to hang out after school. And why wouldn't they? She's one of the nice girls that everyone likes.

But I know how she feels. Right now, it doesn't seem right to have any sort of fun. Not that being trapped inside the house is fun. But sometimes I'll see a picture online that makes me smile, or listen to a song I used to love, and I'll feel guilty. Guilty for enjoying just a single moment of time. Because that's when I remember that Rita lost her life. Then everything comes crashing down again.

I watch the back of Honey's head. Things just haven't been the same since. We're out of sync. Rowena barely speaks to us, rarely showing up to dinner and always hiding in her room. Her bedroom hasn't got a lock, but each evening, I hear her shift her dresser in front of the door. Marigold is quiet, withdrawn. She spends her days looking for jobs online. In the night, I hear her shuffling around downstairs, making endless cups of coffee to fuel midnight painting sessions and her constant sleeplessness. No one says a word about what's going through our heads, but there's not much you miss when you're in the house all day, every day. And if my plan at dinner goes well, then I'll be spending a lot more time in this place.

With Honey ignoring me, I head downstairs. Wilda is in the kitchen, scouring cooking books. There are bags of pasta, flour and rice on the sideboard and the fridge is wide open. She mutters to herself, her eyes darting from open book to open book, occasionally flipping a few pages. I lean on the doorframe, watching her in her frenzy.

"What are you doing?"

Wilda jumps, knocking a bag of flour to the floor. She gasps as white powder goes all over her tights. She throws her hands up in despair and I rush into the kitchen, ducking under the sink to arm myself with the dustpan.

"What a flipping mess I've made," Wilda says, trying to pick up the flour bag without spilling more. I try not to smile at her choice of words. I guess being a teacher has taught her to avoid more vulgar language.

"Sorry to startle you…"

"Don't you worry about it, love. It wasn't your fault," Wilda says breathlessly. She has some flour on the tip of her nose. She puts a hand on her hip. "How's your head?"

I rub the side of my temple. "Yeah. No better, really."

Wilda frowns. She might be the only person who doesn't realise I'm faking. "Maybe we should get the doctor to come again. See what he can do for you."

I ignore the comment, grabbing a brush and sweeping the mess up. 'What are you cooking?'

Wilda stares at the counter. "A good question. I had planned to make a lasagne, but I don't have any pasta sheets...or mince. Or tinned tomatoes. So in short, I was going to cook lasagne, but of course, I have none of the ingredients. Besides, it won't suit Rowena anyway."

I smile. It's moments like this, when she lets go a little, that I see Rita in her.

"Back up plan?"

Wilda chews her thumb, looking sheepish. "Beans on toast?"

I almost roll my eyes before remembering that was something I could only get away with around Rita. With Wilda? I barely know her. I don't want to be rude. I go to the fridge and scan its contents. It's pretty much empty. Wilda blushes.

"I've been a bit strapped for time, I haven't managed to do a shop."

I feel sorry for her. Here she is, the only person in the house working a full time job, and she's still the one trying to cook dinner for five among her other tasks. It occurs to me how different her life must feel too. We've swooped in here and upended her routine. And so far, she's barely seen any gratitude for her trouble.

"It's okay. We can improvise," I say, grabbing a packet of bacon from the fridge. "You know, you should try an online shop. It's so much easier."

"Well I've thought about it, but someone needs to be in to take the order. Living alone before, it was never really a good idea. I'm not really a cook, to be honest. My evening meals are usually microwaveable, not made of individual components."

"You've been doing a good job then," I say. Wilda smiles, ruffling my hair. I resist the urge to flinch away. I know she's only being friendly, but I don't tend to let people touch me if I don't know them very well. I'm not trying to push Wilda away, but I'll need to become more familiar with her before I can get comfortable.

Wilda smiles at me with something like affection. "You're so polite. Rita always said how sweet you are."

The comment makes me want to cry and smile at the same time. It aches. I push the feeling away, returning to the fridge to continue foraging.

"We could make a carbonara. I think you've got everything in."

"Brilliant. We'll do that. Although what about Rowena?"

"She'll have a little pasta without the bacon. And some salad. She's…she's not much of an eater. I can help you make the pasta, if you like?" I smile at her. Perhaps now is a good opportunity to get to know her a little better. Wilda's face lights up.

"Would you? I hate to admit it, but I've never actually cooked a carbonara. Could you show me?"

I nod, already laying out all of the ingredients. I get out a frying pan for the bacon and put some water on to boil. Wilda watches me like a nerdy child in class, taking it all in. I set her cutting up some bacon while I search the cupboard for herbs. Every time I look at Wilda, she's got this goofy grin on her face, as though me being here with her has made her day. Maybe it has. The quiet in the room sets me a little on edge, but I know I shouldn't be scared around her. She's so nice. No adjective could better describe her. She's a nice woman. Maybe that's why she makes me feel more comfortable than most strangers. Besides, she is family. She's Rita's sister. She can't be so bad.

She looks at me and her smile seems to widen even more. She returns to her task of cutting bacon.

"It's so nice having you girls around the house, you know. All quiet as a mouse, the lot of you, but it's good to be around people all of the time. It can get a little lonely, living on your own."

I nod. It's something I know a lot about. It was a long time ago, but I still remember the long nights I would spend awake, waiting for my parents to come home as a kid. Even back in the children's homes, where there was no space or privacy, I preferred it. At least there was always someone around.

"When my husband and I separated, I knew I wouldn't marry again. But I've always liked the idea of having someone to share the house with. What I'm trying to say is...of course it's awful, of course it is. But I feel like Rita has given me such a gift. Sending you girls here."

I frown. "Sending us here?"

Wilda busies herself with putting the bacon in the frying pan. Her cheeks are flushed, and I don't think it's the heat from the pan.

"Oh, you know. I just meant that some good has come out of all of this. She would have wanted you with family, is all. I don't mean to imply that any of this is a good thing…but I appreciate the chance to reconnect. I only wish I'd tried harder sooner. Oh, I don't know. I always mess up what I mean to say."

She does always seems a little skittish. Mostly around me and Rowena. I suppose it's as strange for her as it is for us, living with her two estranged nieces. She's never had the chance to know us. At least not the same way as she knows Mari and Honey. I guess it's hard getting used to calling someone family when they're not your flesh and blood. Kids like me and Rowena – we're not there one day, and then suddenly we are. Standing on your doorstep, dragging along our suitcase of problems and bad memories, expecting to fit in. It's not always that simple. Not for us, and not for them.

"Can I ask you a question, Lori?"

I look up from pouring pasta in the pan. Wilda's smile has slipped a little. Her words have a weight that makes my legs tremble. I know she wants to say something important.

"Okay."

Wilda swallows, wiping her hands on a tea towel. "Are you comfortable here? I...I know now how much you struggle with your anxiety. I think living together has proved that to me. And I just want you to feel safe. In this house…with me. So...are you okay? Do you like living here?"

There are a lot of questions she wants to know the answer to, and all are different. Am I comfortable? Not really. Do I like living here? No, as much as I want to. But am I okay? I turn my head away, unable to meet Wilda's eye.

"I'm better here than I am anywhere else. And I'm so grateful to be here. Really."

The answer seems to satisfy Wilda. She reaches out to squeeze my shoulder. And somehow, impossibly, it feels like her hand is just like Rita's. A reminder that maybe she hasn't left me entirely.

For the first time since we've been living here, it's raining. We've had a good run of sunshine, meaning each night we've spent out on the patio. But tonight, Wilda asks if I'll set the dining room table. The room is a little odd to me. It's clearly not used very often. It's the one room in the house that looks like it could belong to Rita. There are a bunch of cardboard boxes stacked against the wall labelled for a charity sale. The table is covered in Wilda's student's papers, which she tells me to shove in a pile out of the way. On the wall, there are some photographs that I've never seen before. One is of

Wilda's wedding day. She looks stunning, her curls piled on her head in an organised mess. Her dress is knee length, an off-shoulder beauty covered in pale pink flowers. She's laughing in the picture, a hand curled around a glass of champagne as she leans in towards her husband. He holds her free hand, smiling lovingly at her. There's another photograph from her wedding day, but of Wilda and Rita. Their faces are smushed against each other's and they're both grinning. Their curls almost merge so it's not easy to tell where one mop begins and the other ends. I can't help smiling. I stare at the photographs while I set out the cutlery. Where did it all go so wrong for Wilda and Rita?

I can hear the bacon sizzling in the kitchen and the pasta bubbling. Nerves begin to creep in. This dinner is vital. It has to go well. When I enter the kitchen, Wilda is grabbing a bottle of wine from her rack. She examines it, before showing it to me.

"Does Marigold drink white?"

I nod. I'm glad Wilda didn't suggest red. That was always Rita's drink. It pains me how every little thing seems to lead me back to her. I've told myself a million times that making these connections only guarantees me a lifetime of misery. But right now, with the feeling so raw inside me, I can't help it. It's taken me to my lowest point in years. But after everything I've lost, can I be blamed? When you lose someone like Rita, do you ever really recover from that?

I help Wilda take some glasses through to the dining room and finish setting the table. Wilda puts a hand on my back.

"Sit down, dear. I'll call the girls down."

"Are you sure? I can help dish up?" I say, feeling a little desperate. I don't want to sit at the table any longer than I have to. This is going to be hard enough as it is.

"You've done enough, thank you. Make yourself comfortable."

I can't make myself comfortable. I sit down at the head of the table, and then quickly switch seats. I don't want to be the centre of everyone's eyeline. I hear Honey's light feet padding down the stairs first. She gives me a fleeting smile before sitting at the head of the table. I want her next to me – she's usually my most reliable ally, but with her attitude at the moment, I'm more likely to get sympathy from Ro.

Marigold shows up with Rowena right behind her. Something tells me she was forced to the table. She shoves past Marigold to sit beside me, but Mari doesn't even blink an eye. She looks worn down. I suddenly feel guilty. I'm about to add right on top of her pile of worries. But I have to do this. I sink into my seat. I can't back down. Not now.

Wilda reappears, carrying the first plates. She's smiling, oven mitts shrouding her tiny hands.

"You've got Lori to thank for dinner. She saved me in the kitchen."

Rowena stares at her plate, blank faced. "Great. Pasta. Again."

"How about you cook dinner for once then?" Marigold says. Her voice is barely a whisper, but we all hear. Rowena ignores her and stabs at a piece of pasta before the rest of us even have our plates. We all pretend not to notice.

Wilda serves me last and I smile as she sits down beside me. Part of me is hoping she'll take my side. She's so eager to please that I can half believe she might. She catches me looking at her and smiles, a little uncertain. She takes a mouthful of pasta.

"Tastes great, Lori."

Poor Wilda. She's so easy to please. I push my food around my plate. I need to dive right in and tell them what's been keeping me awake all week. I take a deep breath before I can think of a reason to back out.

"I'm not going back to college."

I must've been too quiet, because no one responds. No one even looks up from their plate. My stomach is jittering.

"Mari, I'm not going back to college."

Marigold finally looks up from her plate. She stares at me for a few seconds. Her face is sharp, uninviting.

"You are not quitting college. End of story."

"I wasn't suggesting that. I thought maybe I could study from home."

Mari picks up her fork, stabbing a piece of pasta. "There's no need for that. You'll be better in a few days. You can go back to college when you're ready."

"I can't go back there. I can't even face leaving the house right now. I...I don't think I'm ever going to be ready."

Mari stares at me for a long time. The others are watching too. They all want to know what Marigold will decide. Her face is softer now. She feels sorry for me. And in some ways, that's worse than her being angry. I don't want to be pitied. It reminds me of my inadequacy. It reminds me that I've failed my family. Marigold's eyes flicker to the empty seat left at the table. She's wishing Rita was sitting there, telling her how to react to this. But if Rita was here, she'd be telling me no – and I don't think Marigold can do that to me.

She looks up to the next best thing. Wilda looks surprised that Marigold's asking for her input. She clears her throat, probably wondering what the right answer is.

"Well...Lori isn't a lazy girl. I don't think we need to worry about her slacking off. If we explain to her tutors what her situation is, I'm sure they'd oblige in sending her some notes. I can help a certain amount. If Lori keeps up with her studies, I see no reason why she can't continue them from home. Especially if...if it might improve her mental health."

I can't help blushing. I can't believe we're discussing my mental health at the table. I catch Rowena rolling her eyes, which makes me feel even worse. But I can feel Marigold is hovering on the edge of her decision. She chews her lips and watches me steadily. I keep her gaze, my heart pounding. She sighs, picking up her cutlery again.

"There will be rules."

Honey sighs, shaking her head. I frown. Is she angry at Marigold's decision? Rowena shoves away her bowl as though in protest. My heart is shuddering in my chest. Why does it suddenly feel like they're all against me?

"You'll start seeing a therapist to try and get you better. If your grade slips below a B, you'll return to college. No exceptions. Your Aunt Wilda and I will be discussing this further, but those rules are a good start."

I nod aggressively. I'm not about to start negotiating with her now. I wouldn't want anything to change her mind. Marigold nods, more to herself than to the rest of us. She stands, and I notice that her legs are shaking. She looks in my direction, but avoids my gaze.

"If you don't mind, I need to be excused."

Before any of us can say anything, she leaves the room. Rowena scoffs, shaking her head. Wilda watches her go, looking nervous.

"Do you think one of us should go after her?"

Rowena raises an eyebrow. "Can't you tell she wants to be on her own? Anyone could see that."

Wilda sinks back into her seat a little. "Right. Of course."

Rowena rolls her eyes and stands to leave too. None of us try to stop her. Wilda tries to smile, standing and taking Rowena and Marigold's plates.

"I'll box their food up. They can have it for lunch."

I know no one will touch that food again, but I smile to humour her. As she leaves the room, I look to Honey for her reaction. I catch her looking at me, but she glances away quickly. Her face is stony.

"Honey...are you mad at me?"

She purses her lips, standing too. She's not eaten a bite of her food.

"Put it this way, Lori. We all struggle. Every single one of us in this family. We've all got stuff going on. The difference is, the rest of us get on with it."

LANDING

It's cold sitting on the landing, but right now, it's the only place I feel like being. Everyone's apart. Wilda is watching TV downstairs, and Marigold is in the bath. Honey and Ro are sitting in their rooms. I came out here to escape Honey's frostiness, but sitting here, it's easy to feel the separation in this house.

Not so long ago, I would spend my evenings in the living room. Everyone would be there, even Ro. We'd binge watch our favourite TV shows together, and settle down for our regular favourites on a Saturday night. I can remember Honey skipping parties just to stay with us all, lounging on the sofa with her feet over my lap. It was a time when all of us would be at our most relaxed. Ro would let her guard down, laughing at the rude jokes on chat shows. Sometimes we'd play games and Ro would let her competitive side come out, shouting at Rita when she beat her on MarioKart or ousted her from her winner's seat in Monopoly. We would be up past midnight some days, even when Marigold warned us we'd all be tired for work or school the next day. Now, it's only nine o'clock and none of us can wait to be away from one another.

I hear the bathroom door open downstairs and the padding of Marigold's feet on the wooden floor, heading to the living room.

"Eavesdropping?"

I jump, my heart lurching. Rowena chuckles, pleased with herself.

"You scared the shi...life. You scared the life out of me."

"Oh, wow. Did Little Miss Perfect almost slip up and say a rude word? Things must be bad."

I lean my face against the bannister. I want to roll my eyes, but it somehow feels too aggressive. That's her style, not mine. "I'm not perfect. Far from it."

"No? So why does everyone treat you like some precious being? Like you're too good for this world? Everyone tucks you up in bubble wrap, Lori."

"You don't."

"Hmm?"

"You don't think I'm precious. You don't wrap me up in bubble wrap."

Rowena rolls her eyes, unwrapping chewing gum from her hoodie pocket. "No. I think you're babied. I think it's ridiculous."

At least she's honest. Rowena rips the paper her gum came in, serrating the edges. "I'm not saying you don't have a tough time. I'm not heartless. But come on. Rita would have never let this shit lie. Dropping out of college? It's a step back for you."

"Five steps. You think I like it any more than the rest of you?"

"You're the one who suggested it. Hey, maybe I'll tell Marigold I've caught anxiety off you. Then I won't have to go back to school."

It hurts a little, when Rowena or Honey act like I'm making a fuss. It's like they think I'm weaving an endless lie into my life. Making things difficult for myself. Maybe they think I do it for attention. But Rowena of all people should know that life doesn't work like that. When you're drowning, you call for help any way you can. Yes, you want to be noticed. But not so that people pity you.

So that they save you.

Maybe Rowena's forgotten what it's like to be saved. But I haven't.

"Why don't you want to go back? Is school that bad?"

Rowena stares at her lap. "You know how it is. It's school."

I nod. School's tough for anyone. But when you're a lost soul like Rowena? It's hell. Back home, she at least had a few friends. The kind of friends that laughed at her crass jokes and didn't care that she was a misfit. But here? It's a small town. Maybe she's not found someone she can get on with.

"It's early days. You could still make friends."

"Everyone already has friends. No one wants to hang out with some loser."

"You're not a loser."

"Yeah? Well, I'm not a winner. When have I ever got to keep something good?"

It's so casual the way she says it. Like it's usual to have your life ripped apart on a regular basis. I watch her, hiding behind her dark fringe. I don't know a lot about what happened to Rowena before she was fostered by Rita and Marigold. She had parents. They were around. That pretty much guarantees that they were scumbags, that they did something bad enough to have Rowena taken from them. We must have similarities in our past, though we don't ever talk about life before we were adopted. Sometimes, I think maybe she handled it better than me. But maybe she's just keeping all that hurt inside. Maybe that's the only way she knows how to survive.

"Things will pick up."

"Like they have for you?"

I can't help rolling my eyes now. She has an answer for everything. I keep my back to her, staring through the bannister to the living room. I can see the TV flickering. Wilda's watching some late-night chat show. But I watch as Marigold shuffles through to the living room, and within moments, the TV is muted. Rowena leans in with me, listening. Someone is gasping for breath. Then follows a hushing, like the whispers of the sea. It's a familiar sound. I try to place where I've heard it. When I realise, my heart stops.

It's the sound of panic attacks. Of Rita comforting me in my room where I'd locked myself away, ashamed of my fear. It was the sound I'd wake to after a nightmare, the sound that swallowed my screams and squashed them flat, until the only thing left was Rita hushing me, soothing me. And then when I was calmer, the hush would become a hum of one of her favourite songs, or something she'd heard on the radio. And when I heard that, I knew it was safer.

I don't realise I'm standing until my feet reach the top of the stairs.

"Where are you going?" Rowena hisses, but I ignore her. I'm drawn to the sound of Wilda comforting

Marigold. I need to know. I need to know whether she's the same as Rita.

I seem to sink into every stair as I try not to creak on my descent. Marigold's sobs are muffled, and I see that her head is buried in Wilda's lap like a child. Wilda strokes her hair with a smooth, long motion. I touch the back of my head. I can almost feel Rita's hands mimicking her sister's movements.

I crouch in the hallway, my back against the wall so I have a good place to listen. I can even see a little. Rowena stares at me, before shaking her head and retreating to her room. As Marigold's sobs begin to subside, Wilda's hushing descends into a hum. I shiver, the sound so familiar. Somehow, as she hums, her pearly tone has lowered, almost identical to the husk of Rita's voice. Marigold sinks into her, her body limp.

"I'm doing everything wrong. I'm a bad mother."

"You're not." She's succinct. To the point.

Just like Rita.

"I am. I keep making such bad decisions. I should have made her go back to college."

"You can't force her. She's not a child anymore."

"No, but she can't make these decisions for herself. If she was allowed to do everything she wanted to, she'd never do anything. That's why Rita was so good for her. She brought her out of her shell. Got her to do things she didn't want to do. I could never persuade her in that way. I just gave in to her."

She makes me sound like a child having a tantrum. It stings, hearing her talk about me this way. But I guess she's not wrong. She was always the relief from Rita, if I needed it. The one I could hide behind if things became too much. I appreciated that of her. I thought it was because she knew my boundaries – how much of Rita's pushing I could take. Now, I see that she just couldn't deny me my wishes. That she was letting Rita lead the way because she hadn't figured out how to.

"I just can't help thinking...it must have been so awful. Being there, when it happened. I can understand why she's scared. She's had such a tough life. But if the roles were reversed...if I had taken her out that day instead...or we had let her stay in, like she wanted...everything would have been better."

"You can't think like that."

"But I do. If I was dead, and Rita was alive...nothing would be falling apart."

I gasp so hard it catches in my throat. It's a miracle Mari and Wilda don't hear me. Does Mari really think we'd be fine, if she had died instead of Rita? I feel guilt stabbing at my chest. Yes, Rita and I had a special relationship. Yes, Rita mattered more than anything in the world to me. But Marigold has my heart too. If she was gone in Rita's place, I'd still be falling apart. We all would. And the more I think about it, the more I think Rita would've fallen apart the hardest.

"You're not thinking straight, sweetie. I know you're struggling without her. And I know how parenting is different for two women. People expect different things from you. But you both did such an incredible job. You and Rita were just different in your approaches. You brought different things to the table when it came to parenting. It doesn't make you any better or worse than one another."

"But I can't do anything right. Rowena can't stand me. Honey is so reserved, and Lori…"

"Mari...you're all going through one of the toughest things a family can endure. No one expects you to be perfect at a time like this."

74

"But I should be able to support them. I should know what to do, what to say. And I keep thinking, with Lori...I just don't know if I'm doing the right thing, letting her stay at home. I need Rita here. I need her to tell me how to be." My stomach twists as Marigold sniffs again. "Rita would know what to do. She always did. She understood Lori, you know? No one would know she was adopted, looking at the pair of them together. They clicked. But me and her…"

My chest tightens. I want to go to her and tell her. Tell her that I never loved her any less, just because we're polar opposites. Just because she is different to Rita, to Honey, to Rowena. I want to tell her that I love them all with everything I have in me.

But I don't.

"I know I've been distant in the past few years…I know that I'm only just beginning to learn the dynamics of this family…but those kids love you to death, Marigold, I can tell. You're so lucky to have them. And when it comes to Ro, to Lori…they're special. Because they know what it's like to have a hard life. They know what it looks like when someone lets them down. And that's how I know that you're doing just fine. They dote on you. They show it in different ways, but they do. They see what you've done for them, how you've saved them. Don't be so hard on yourself. They'll never forget how your love changed their lives."

There are tears falling down my cheeks. Wilda summed it up better than I ever could've done. As I creep back up the stairs, wiping my face, I know Wilda will tell Marigold what she needs to hear. Sometimes, it's hard to voice the things that she was saying. I don't like to talk about the past when it's only ever held hardship for me. But Rita and Mari changed all of that. Maybe I don't give them enough credit for that. Now that Rita is gone, things will be different.

But even with her gone, I haven't lost my family.

STUDY

Today has been my first official day at home, and it's been uneventful, as I had hoped. Marigold has been in her bedroom for most of the day. Wilda's teaching, and then staying behind for a meeting with a troublesome kid's parents. Honey finally took up an offer from someone from college to hang out, so she's going to be home later. Rowena should be home by four. Me? I've spent all day quietly getting on with my work. And that suits me just fine.

Wilda has given me use of her study during the day, and I've loved every second in here. It's the kind of office I've always envisioned having, with cork boards and shelves of books and a wallet of fine tip coloured pens on the desk. It's the perfect writing hub. It takes me the morning to skim over the notes for my other classes, and then I turn my attention to writing.

Mrs Wickham sent us a series of prompts to look through. Our first task of the semester is to write something inspired by one of them, but I've never been much good at working from prompts. I've tried it a couple of times when I've been feeling uninspired, but it's never worked for me. Images don't prompt much for me either. All of the techniques that writers are supposed to follow just bring me grinding to a halt. Panic starts to set in. The deadline is this afternoon. I have to get to work if I want to submit on time.

Surely she won't mind if I stray from the prompts...I open the short story I've been working on. It's kind of gritty – an ode to my anxiety. It's the sort of thing I would hate to read. I don't like anything that doesn't have a happy ending. But writing is different. It's an outlet. It's taking my feelings outside of me for a while, and throwing them into something raw that I write. Usually afterwards, I can't bear to read it over, not even to edit. But it takes the edge off for a while. It makes me feel better.

My hands hover over the keys. The story is near the end, but it needs something. Something to send the reader tumbling off the edge. The way I've done a million times on the days where panic engulfs me. I close my eyes. The keys are so familiar to me I don't even have to look to know where each letter stands. I sink into the prose. It's like muscle memory. My fingers do most of the work. My mind works in the background, interweaving the words rhythmically like a thread through fabric. It's so familiar that it feels stranger to stop than to carry on. When I finish, I feel the way you do when you finish a good book, or watch the series finale of your favourite show...

What now?

I stare at the story for a while and the writer's doubt begins to set in. Is this story realistic? Does it make sense? Are the characters strong? Are they likeable? But most importantly, is this good enough to send to a teacher? I glance up at the clock. I have an hour to write something else if I want to. But nothing good can come from a rushed job.

I sit for a while, staring at the screen. When I glance at the clock, fifteen minutes have passed. I need to send it soon, or I'll be reprimanded. I can't risk that – Marigold made the rules very clear. If I want to study from home, I have to prove it won't affect my grades. Which means actually turning in my work.

I attach the file to the email and write a bumbling message about why I didn't use one of the prompts and how sorry I am to waste Mrs Wickham's time. My heart is wild as I reach for the button, but I can't seem to press it. I close my eyes. *Just let your body take over for a while and press the button. You're overthinking. Pretend you're writing. When you write, you're not afraid.*

Two minutes before the deadline, I press send.

I have dinner in the oven when everyone arrives home. Honey looks a little surprised when she sees me. I'm dressed for the first time in a week. Freshly showered, and wearing my favourite perfume. I even painted my nails while I was waiting for dinner to cook. I've poured everyone's favourite drinks and set them by their place mats, and there's a bowl of fresh salad close to where Rowena will sit. Wilda enters the room, her head tilting upwards to sniff the air.

"Is that chicken I smell, Lori?"

I nod shyly. "I made pesto chicken and rice. I hope it's okay."

"Lovely! I could get used to this…"

Rowena arrives, a scowl already set on her face, but she softens a little when she sees the salad on the table. She takes her seat without a word, but I can tell she's pleased to be catered for. The others follow suit, though Mari is still missing. I haven't seen her all day. I check on the chicken and then head upstairs to see what she's doing. When I open the door to her room, it's dark. Marigold is curled up on top of her duvet, fast asleep. I close the door quietly and leave the room. This is the most sleep she's had in weeks. I don't want to be the one to disturb her.

I dish up the rest of the food and take it through to Honey, Ro and Wilda. Wilda looks delighted as I put a plate in front of her.

"Delicious. Will Marigold be joining us?"

"She's taking a nap. I thought it was best to let her sleep…"

Wilda nods sympathetically. "Yes, of course. We can just make do with the four of us."

I sit down at the head of the table. Honey catches my eye and smiles. I smile back. It's nice that she's stopped her freezing out act, even if she hasn't apologised. I don't need an apology to forgive her – I'm just glad to have her back. She cuts her chicken delicately.

"How was your first day at home, Lori?"

I blush. I don't like the attention on me at dinner. But I'm in a good mood – I don't mind talking about that.

"It was pretty great. I managed to catch up on most of my notes. It's surprising how little an hour's teaching amounts to on paper. In some ways, it's quicker and easier to read it yourself. I've done some sample questions in advance. There's a test coming up next week, so I'll be prepared in no time."

Honey blinks. "You make it sound like doing A Levels is easy."

"It's not easy. But it's easier for me than in a classroom. I've never been able to concentrate properly in a school setting. I end up spending half my time with crippling anxiety and miss what the teacher is saying. Now, I have a lot of time to dedicate to each subject with no distractions. I don't have to spend two hours on the bus either, which helps. But I spent most of today on my Creative Writing project anyway."

"Well how did that go?" Wilda chips in. "It sounds like such a fun subject. A relief from learning about psychology, I would imagine?"

"Yeah, in some ways, though psychology is pretty interesting. I feel like it helps me understand the way my brain is wired. As for the writing…it's not easy, but I enjoy it a lot. I'm just scared my teacher won't like what I've written."

"Well I'm sure she has no reason to dislike it! What makes you say that?"

Every fibre of my being I think. "I don't know. Just paranoia, I suppose. It takes me over."

"Well, I'm sure she'll love what you have written. And if not, you can only improve, right?"

She's right, but it's not really what I want to hear. I want Mrs Wickham to be impressed. Not many people have ever read my writing. I used to show Rita the occasional story, but no one else. Not even Marigold. Now that I'm sharing my work with a teacher, who is professionally hired to teach Creative Writing, I'm scared. She knows what she's talking about. She doesn't have to pretend to like what I write the way Rita could easily have done. I'm suddenly put off my dinner. Wilda starts asking Honey some questions about college and I sit quietly, trying to think of anything but my studies.

As the others are finishing up with their dinner, there's a knock on the front door. Wilda frowns, wiping her mouth with a napkin.

"Is someone expecting a guest?"

Honey and Rowena exchange a glance, shaking their heads. I begin to clear the plates from the table. I'm not expecting company, of course. Everyone I know is in the house.

As I'm stacking the dishwasher, I hear Wilda answering the door. I hear a woman's voice from the door that seems somewhat familiar, but I can't place it. Wilda tells the woman to come inside and gives her directions to the kitchen. I freeze. It could be anyone. I place the last plate in the dishwasher with shaking hands. I don't like strangers coming into the house. It makes me nervous. But when I look up, I see a familiar face.

"Mrs Wickham?"

She looks as stern as when I last saw her, and I immediately wonder if I'm in trouble for some reason. I blink twice to make sure I'm not imagining her. What is she doing here?

"Good evening, Lori. It's good to see you're a little better. You gave me a fright in class. I hope you don't mind me dropping by. I've got something to discuss with you, since you won't be coming into classes. I did email your mother in advance of me coming…"

I fidget, playing with the hem of my t-shirt for something to do. Marigold must've fallen asleep before she told me about this. Mrs Wickham turns to raise an eyebrow to Wilda.

"Is there somewhere Lori and I can have a little chat?"

"If you like, Lori can show you to my study. She's been using it for homework."

"Perfect. Come on, dear. Lead the way."

My legs wobble as I lead Mrs Wickham up the stairs. Just when I thought I'd escaped college, Mrs Wickham has brought it to my home. What can she possibly want? Then it dawns on me.

She didn't like my writing. She's going to tell me I'm not right for the course. My stomach twists. I know I'm being silly. She can't kick me out of a class – even if I'm terrible, it's her job to help me get better. But I have a horrible feeling about this meeting. She made the effort to come all the way here. That can't be a good thing.

I lead Mrs Wickham into the study and she looks around, nodding in approval.

"A lovely workspace. It's clear that you're better here than in the classroom. Do you feel inspired in your surroundings?"

I blink several times. "I...I hadn't thought about it."

"Maybe you should. Half of the art of writing is being in the right place at the right time. That's when magic happens. Please, take a seat. We have a lot to discuss, and I hope to be home by nine to catch up on Corrie."

I feel a little better once I'm sat down, but not much. I'm still scared of what Mrs Wickham has to say. She perches on the spare chair in the corner. She threads her fingers together and rests her hands on her knees. I swallow. She looks like she means business.

"Mrs Wickham...I'm sorry that I strayed from the prompts. I should have stuck to the task. I didn't mean-"

"Oh please, Lori. Don't worry about it. Those prompts were something I spent five minutes researching on the web. I'm not offended."

"You're...you're not?"

"Of course not. It's just a nudge for the students who take on this subject as an easy ride. It gets them writing, even if what they come up with is absolute rubbish." Mrs Wickham taps her head. "But you don't need that. You use your brain. You have experiences to draw on, don't you?"

I struggle for words, but Mrs Wickham isn't looking at me. She takes out a pile of papers from her bag and shuffles through them, showing me the pages.

"You see that? You see all of those pages, covered in red scribbles?"

I nod, confused. Mrs Wickham shoves most of the papers back in her bag.

"Those are the students I marked from my other Creative Writing class. A class of very little imagination. Some potential is there, if they make the effort. But very little creativity. I've filled their pages with notes they probably won't bother to read. Now, here's your feedback. I don't normally mark so quickly, but I was interested to read your work. I read it during my free period this afternoon."

Mrs Wickham hands back my story. It takes a minute for my eyes to focus on the paper with nerves clouding my vision, but when I do, I see a page filled with obnoxiously large ticks and smiley faces. I look up at her in disbelief.

"You liked it?"

"Darling, I adored it. It was a very powerful piece. Full of raw emotion. You need some work on structure, but the writing itself is spot on. Very powerful stuff, Lori. Very powerful."

I flick through the other pages. There are several illegible comments in large looped writing, but mostly, all I see is ticks. I can't help but smile. I cover my mouth with my hand, not wanting Mrs Wickham to think me smug, but she shakes her head at me.

"Take pride in what you've done, Lori. You clearly have very little confidence in your own abilities, but you deserve to revel in this success."

I let my hand drop, grinning. This is the best I've felt in a long time. But something tells me Mrs Wickham wouldn't come all this way just to tell me she liked my story. I look at her expectantly. She clears her throat.

"I've been teaching this course for a few years now. Every now and then, I see a sliver of stardust and I can't resist. I want to take you under my wing. Not just as my student, but also as more than that. I want to be able to coach you further. What I'm saying is that I want you to send me work as often as possible. Anything you write, I want to see it. I want to guide you along your way because I believe you can produce something really special, given the time and resources."

I stare at the pieces of paper in front of me, wondering how one piece of writing could trigger all of this.

"I'll help you with other things too, like getting yourself noticed online, or finding an agent, or entering suitable competitions. I just want to know that your heart is in this. I don't like to waste time on students who don't really want something. I like to see passion and drive. Do you think you have that? Is that something you can offer?"

I don't know how to respond. Of course, I want to say yes. But part of me is afraid. What if I let her down? What if this piece of writing was a one off masterpiece, and the rest of my stories are rubbish? Mrs Wickham is watching me intently, waiting for me to speak. She pats my knee.

"Lori, I'm telling you this now. I'm not the best writer in the world, but I know the writer's world better than anyone. This could be really good for you. I'd hate to see you pass up an opportunity that could change everything for you. So. What do you say?"

I'm smiling again. My eyes are cloudy with tears as I look up, but for once, they're happy tears. "I say yes."

PORCH

Staying at home suits me just fine. The past few days, I've felt my anxieties dull to a manageable level, and I've been able to focus on my studies. Each day, I work until midday, have a little lunch, spend the afternoon writing, and then have time to make dinner for the family. It's the perfect setup, and everyone's mood seems to have improved since. Rowena isn't trying to fight with everyone anymore, Marigold is tentatively getting used to having me around all day, and Wilda seems relieved that everyone is holding themselves together. It's been a good thing for all of us.

But I haven't forgotten Marigold's terms and conditions for allowing me to stay at home. Somehow, as I hear her coming up the stairs, I know she's about to bring up therapy. She sticks her head around my bedroom door, fixing me with a maternal look.

"I think it's time we had a chat about finding you a therapist."

"I'm kind of in the middle of homework…"

"I appreciate that, but we had an agreement. Staying at home means you see someone about your mental health. Waiting for your problems to go away isn't going to cut it. We need to organise a day and a time."

"You may as well pick. I'm not going anywhere. Whatever suits."

"Lori, come on. We haven't properly spoken about it. Let's have a quick chat, and then I'll let you get back to your work."

I try not to sigh. I don't want to be cheeky. And though talking about therapy is the last thing I want to discuss, I've been waiting for Marigold to come to me. We haven't spoken much since we arrived here. Not properly. I put my laptop on the floor and Marigold sits at the end of my bed, legs crossed. She looks a little like her old self today. She's swapped her plaid pyjamas for her floaty pink trousers, and the anklet Rita bought her for their ten-year anniversary is looped around her leg. It's almost as though she tried to pull herself together for the purpose of this conversation. She tucks her hair behind her ears, and I catch the scent of lavender. It's like a punch to the stomach, but Marigold seems unaffected by it.

"You must know by now that I'm worried about you. It's not a healthy way to live, never leaving the house. I know it's only been a week, but I already see changes in you. You look pale."

I think she must be imagining it. My skin doesn't look any different to me. I think that's a Mum thing – they spend so much time worrying for their children that they see issues that aren't there.

"Mum...I'm as happy as I can be right now. I feel better, knowing I don't have to worry. I'm just...I'm taking time to heal. And it's easier when I don't have to think about every single external factor too. You know how I feel about…well, everything."

Marigold cups my face tenderly. Her hand is trembling. "I know, baby. I just don't want this to consume you. I don't want you to live your life in fear. What happened to Rita was...a horrible accident. Things like that...they're not supposed to happen."

There's a lump in my throat that I can't seem to shift. I hang my head. "But it *did* happen. Like it always seems to when I'm around. Something always goes wrong."

"Oh, Lori…"

"When I stepped out of the house that day, every instinct in me told me it was a bad idea. That I should stay home. And I know what you'll say – that I feel that way every day. Which is exactly why I can't do this anymore. Because going out there, I put myself at risk again. If I ignore my instincts…then what else will go wrong? I…I can't lose anyone else. Here, at least I'm safe. It's better to be stuck here than have something outside ruin everything else again."

Marigold stares at me and for a moment, I see myself through her eyes. A kid who is so terrified by life that she refuses to participate in it. Her eyes soften and she pats my leg.

"You know what? When you put it like that, it doesn't seem so ludicrous."

Marigold lets the subject of therapy lie for a few days. I keep on with my routine, finding my rhythm with life. The weekend arrives and I stay in while my sisters make other plans. Rowena has met a few people at school, so she plans to meet them in town. Honey is going to the local library for a change of scenery. Marigold is keeping to her room, painting in the hours when she's awake. I just carry on with my new version of normal, spending my morning studying to keep up with my homework. By midday, I'm done and ready to relax.

I'm in the kitchen eating lunch when I hear the knock at the door. My fork pauses over my chicken salad. The knock is insistent and rhythmical, like the person is knocking a tune. I half hope that Marigold will get up and answer the door, but I suspect she's asleep, and everybody else is out. I stand up to answer the door, hoping the person is just dropping off a package or something. But when I open the door to the porch, I stop in my tracks..

It's the girl from the bus. The one who sat in front of me in class. The one that made my heart skip a beat. She's peering through the glass of our porch, and when she sees me, she waves and grins as though we're best friends. Today, she's wearing a green satin dress with a turtleneck jumper. It's cool in an effortless way, just like the rest of her. It seems like the sort of thing only she could pull off. She looks like she belongs in an autumn issue of a clothing catalogue. She even smells like autumn air when I open the door. But I only have one question – why is she here?

"Hi! I'm Vanessa, from across the street! Mum found out you guys were moving in with Wilda, and I wanted to come and say hello, but she told me to wait until you guys had settled in...I figured it's been long enough now, right? God, it's exciting to have someone young move into this neighbourhood! I don't think I've seen another person pre-menopause on this road since I've lived here…" She stops for a moment to take a breath, and she meets my eye. She grins at my startled expression. "Sorry, I tend to ramble. I should come with a warning sign or something. Or a badge that says 'I never shut up, run for the hills!' I tend to keep talking until someone stops me. Or I run out of breath. But that doesn't happen often. Please, interrupt me before I talk your ear off again."

I blink several times, trying to figure out if she's real. She's grinning at me.

"You'll get used to that."

"I...don't know which part of that to respond to first."

She laughs. "How about we start with your name?"

For whatever reason, I blush. It doesn't take much for me, but I feel like Vanessa is the type of girl to really bring out the colour of my cheeks. "Lori."

"Lori...where have I heard that name…" She stares at me for a few moments before something clicks. "Oh my goodness! You were in my class. I remember you fainting. Is that why you haven't been back to college? Oh gosh, sorry. That's a rude question. Forget I asked. Can I come in?"

I shift awkwardly from one foot to the other. "Wilda isn't actually here…"

"Oh, that's okay! I'm actually here to see you and your sisters. I thought it would be cool if we got to know each other! I've been waiting for you guys to move in, like, forever. I mean, not you guys literally, but someone my age, you know? It gets pretty lonely around here, especially since we live so far out from the college. I barely ever get to see my friends after classes!" Vanessa pauses. "Oh. Sorry. Off on one again. So? May I?"

Words fail me, but I manage to shuffle away from the door to allow Vanessa inside. She strolls into the house and through to the kitchen, where she flicks the kettle on and gets out a mug. I blink in surprise. Vanessa covers her mouth, stifling a giggle.

"Sorry. I'm on autopilot. I come here a lot. Wilda is usually happy for me to make myself at home. I hope that doesn't bother you."

"No, I...it just took me by surprise."

"Of course, you guys have been here for a few weeks now, and you haven't seen me, so it must seem a little strange me showing up here. I've been coming to Wilda for tuition for years. We're fast friends."

"That's…that's great.'"

"So you're Wilda's niece? I met Honey once, when she came to visit. You've got such a lovely big family. It's just my Mum and Dad at home. But I suppose you're a full house!"

Not quite. Not without Rita. I wonder how much this girl knows. Does she know that Rita's gone? I decide that she doesn't, but I'm not about to bring it up. "Yeah. It's nice. After...it's nice to have a family again."

Vanessa's face flickers with recognition for a moment, but she replaces her pity with a smile. She must sense that family is a touchy subject right now. She plops a tea bag in a mug.

"Tea?"

"No thanks. I don't drink it."

Vanessa taps her temple. "I'll remember that. Coffee? Hot squash? No! Wait! I've got it." She closes her eyes, clicking her fingers as though words have escaped her. Her eyes snap open. "Caramel hot chocolate. Marshmallows, no cream."

I can't help smiling. "Woah. You're good."

Vanessa takes an exaggerated bow. Her eyes sparkle when she smiles. "It's your favourite. I have a knack for guessing."

My heart skips a beat. "Is that...is that a reference to *Chocolat*?"

Vanessa's grinning now. "I thought you might get it. Like I said. I have a knack for guessing."

"That's...that's one of my favourite books."

"Tell me about it. I wrote an entire essay on it for my English class. And let me tell you, Mrs Wickham was not impressed when I turned in a short story about chocolate. She thinks I'm obsessed."

"Maybe you are a little."

"And what?" Vanessa grins, spooning powdered hot chocolate into a mug that says *Best Teacher* on it. "It's the little things, isn't it? That make life good. Like waking up before your alarm and having ten more minutes to sleep."

"Using a new pen for the first time."

"Spoken like a true writer. New notebooks are good, too. Ooh, I've got another. Friday feeling."

"When a trailer for the adaptation of your favourite book is released."

Vanessa cocks her head to the side, grinning. "Nerd."

"And proud."

"Join the club."

It's only when the conversation pauses that I realise how easy it's flowing. It shocks me. Usually, I would be a nervous mess. But something about Vanessa makes me feel comfortable. I can tell she's the kind of girl that will carry the conversation if it lags, but even so, people like that can put me on edge. When I feel I have nothing to say, I'm scared of being boring. But me and Vanessa seem to have hit it off right away. Or maybe she's just being polite. But I find that I don't mind. At least I have someone to talk to.

Vanessa hands me my mug, marshmallows and all. I bring the mug close to my face and breathe in the sweet smell of the chocolate. I take a sip and let the warmth fill me up. Vanessa watches me, sipping her own drink.

"Is my hot chocolate worthy of your approval?"

"The marshmallow to hot chocolate ratio is perfect."

"I'm glad you think so. Since you're new around here, I'll bet you've never been to Rococo's, have you? They do the best hot chocolate. It's actually divine. They have, like, a million flavours. I like the chocolate orange one personally, but I'm sure they could whip you up a good caramel hot chocolate. Especially if I ask for you. I'm their best customer, they don't refuse me much. So? Do you fancy it some day?"

I waver. How am I supposed to tell his wonderful, attractive girl that I can't go for hot chocolate with her? How am I supposed to tell her that I'm too scared to leave the house?

"Well...I'm sure I'll have time at some point."

Vanessa raises an eyebrow, still smiling. "Yeah? Is this a playing hard to get act?"

I try for a laugh, hoping she's just teasing. "You could call it that."

"Well just let me know when you're free. I have student council meetings on Mondays, but they always finish pretty early. Then again, it takes forever to get home in rush hour, so...maybe not Mondays. I have a writer's group on Wednesday's so I'm always busy then. Hey! You write, right? Ha. That's hard to say. But you could come along!"

I'm panicking now. That's two invitations I'll have to turn down. "I don't know...I'm not that confident about people reading my work."

I hold my breath, but fortunately, Vanessa looks pretty understanding. "Say no more. But just know, if you ever want an editor, I'm your girl. You can send me your stuff any time. I love to read fiction or poetry that my friends write. Let's swap numbers! I get the feeling that we'll be hanging out a lot more now."

I doubt it. My heart sinks, but at least she's not running for the hills. She wants to see me again. I hand Vanessa my phone and she inputs her number, her face screwed up in the concentration of remembering it.

"I'll have to pop over some other day when the others are home too." She hands me my phone back. "The ball's in your court, Lori. You've got my number." She drains her tea with a smile, steam still rising from the mug. "I'd better dash. I was actually meant to be picking up some packages for my Mum, but I thought I'd come and introduce myself as a detour. I'll see you around!"

"Yeah...I'll be here."

She surprises me by throwing her arms around me and I stumble, laughing. Her soft blonde hair tickles my face. My arms stay stiff at my side, trapped by her embrace, but I like that she's hugging me. It makes my heart beat a little faster.

"Sorry. I'm a hugger. I should have mentioned."

"It's okay. I...I don't mind."

Vanessa is grinning again when she pulls away. She waggles her fingers at me and then bounds for the door. At this point, it doesn't even surprise me to see her walking with such a bounce in her step – it's clearly her complete vibe. I stand in the porch watching her go and think that after only ten minutes, I might be a little in love with the girl.

MARIGOLD'S ROOM

The house is quiet. Too quiet. I strain my ears in search of noise as I stand in the kitchen, a bowl of cereal in my hand. The only noise is the crackling of my cereal in the milk. I scoop a spoonful into my mouth, but being able to hear myself eating is even worse than the silence. I decide that some music might help, and I fumble for my phone to scroll through Vanessa's playlists. Since she came over the other day, she's managed to scout me out on every social media site possible, but I still haven't found the courage to text her. The thought of her distracts me for a moment as I press play on her 'road trip' playlist, but then I'm back to looking up at the ceiling. Somewhere above me, Marigold is in her room, silent as a mouse. It makes me nervous, thinking of her in there alone. I know the dangers of people locked behind closed doors. I know what that can do to a person – how it can destroy you. Closing doors closes your mind too. It leaves you closed to the possibility of a better time, a better life. When you close a door for too long, the lock gets jammed and there's no escape.

Just as I'm thinking I should check on her, her door creaks open and I hear her coming downstairs. She looks even more tired than when she went in. I'm certain she must have slept today since I heard her up all night, but she doesn't give the impression that she's well rested. She tries for a smile while she makes coffee with shaking hands, her hair seemingly greasy though she washed it last night. When I ask what she'd like for dinner, she says she's not hungry. I lean on the counter, watching the remnants of the strong woman I knew falling apart.

I need to talk to her. In this house, she's become someone I don't recognise, but I know she's in there somewhere. No one can lose themself that quickly. But I know what to do.

I watch Marigold glide into the living room, settling down in front of the TV. She sips her coffee with a blank expression and I use it as an opportunity to sneak upstairs.

I need to see what she's been painting.

Her room is a mess. The bed is unmade, and the quilt is scattered with paint tubes. The room smells a little sour, like crayons and sweat, the fumes from undried paint clogging the room up. Normally, Marigold likes to paint with the windows open, but today, the curtains are closed and there's definitely no fresh air getting in.

The canvas she's working on is propped up on an easel. It's one I've seen before, way back before we came to live with Wilda. It's mostly pencil lines right now, but some of it is painted, starting in the bottom right corner of the canvas. Marigold has always said that she likes to start painting from the smallest point and work outwards. She says that way, the bulk of the hard work is in the middle, but by then you're already kick-started. Then, when it comes to finishing, the task doesn't seem so mammoth as the task shrinks into the opposite corner.

There's something different about the picture now. Not just the fact that it's made more progress since I last saw it. But the colours have shifted. It's a scene I recognise – it's of a cove we visited once on holiday in a town called Criccieth. It's one of those towns that looks like it's straight out of a fairy tale, complete with a castle on a hill and a pebble beach. It rained the whole time we were there, naturally, but it's hard to ignore beauty, even when the whole sky seems to be pouring down on top of you.

Mari started out with light paints, every colour mixed with a dab of white until the scene seemed to be rose tinted. But now, the colours have melted into night. Murky waters lap against sand as dark as soil. Where the sun had once been rising above the waves, grubby pencil marks have been hastily erased. Now, a dull moon hangs low over the water, no light emitting from it. There's something new stencilled in as well. It's so small I almost don't see it, and I think that's the point. In the middle of the sea, there's a figure. A woman, I think, her hands reaching towards the sky. I trace her with my finger, my heart dropping to my stomach. Is this meant to be Marigold?

"Do you like it?"

I jump, turning to see Marigold standing behind me, still holding her coffee. I expect her to be angry – she believes personal space is one of the most important things a person can possess – but her face is soft. She stands next to me, looking at the painting with her ever-critical eye.

"I...I'm not sure."

Marigold's lips twist as she examines her work. "It turned out differently to how I planned at the start. But a lot has changed since then."

I nod. Marigold looks worn down as she reaches for my hand. I take it and relish the gesture. It makes me feel like the connection we've lost is back. Even if only for a moment. Marigold closes her eyes.

"I'm not coping, Lori. This isn't how life is supposed to go. We were supposed to have a happily ever after."

"I know."

Marigold pulls me in to her and I lean my head against her shoulder, trying not to let the tears surface. This moment isn't about my pain. It's about supporting Marigold through hers. She sniffs.

"At least I've got my girls. I've got you, haven't I?"

"Of course you do."

Marigold nods and then pulls away, wiping a tear from her eyes. They're rubbed raw from her tired hands pawing at them so often. Marigold guides me by my arm to her bed and sits me down.

"Can you keep a secret, Lori?"

I'm suddenly nervous. What secrets can she possibly have? But I nod because I don't know how else to respond. Marigold's hands are shaking as she shifts them under her pillow, searching for something. When her hands resurface, she's holding an envelope. She holds it close to her heart for a few moments, her eyes closed. Then she fixes her gaze on me, looking determined.

"I had to tell someone. I thought...I knew it should be you. You were so close with Rita. You'll understand what I have to do."

"Mum...you're scaring me."

Marigold pats my leg. "You'll understand once you've read the letter."

I hold the envelope with caution. I don't want to dirty the envelope with my fingers – this is sacred. Something that Rita once held. The envelope has already been opened, of course, but still, I plan to treat it with respect. With Marigold's gaze urging me to open it, I take out the letter and begin to read.

Marigold,

When you told me you had a fear of death, I asked you why. You told me that in death, there's nothing. That you would never see me or our children again. That we'd never hear each other speak again. You told me that you feared that we'd have a fight and die without making up, or that we wouldn't have a chance to say goodbye. If you're reading this, I'm not here any longer. If you're reading this, we need a chance to say goodbye properly.

I've made 'The List.' For each year that we live in each other's company, I'll add something to the list to be completed. You must complete everything on the list, no matter how much it scares you. That was the deal. And every step of the way, reach into yourself and find me. I promise I'll be there each step of the way.

All my love.

Rita

I look up at Marigold. She smiles sadly at me.

"We made a pact. We were young. We'd been together for a year or so. Tip-toeing around, trying not to let anyone know we were together. It was exhausting. It was sad. It hurt the both of us, not being able to tell anyone about our relationship. Rita made me promise her something – she said that one day, we had to be confident enough to do anything we wanted to do. Even the things that scared us. And that's when she wrote the list."

I turn the page over, and there it is. The list of things to complete.

1. *Skinny dipping*
2. *Volunteer for a charity abroad*
3. *Have children*
4. *Go skydiving for charity*
5. *Run a marathon*
6. *Go to a reunion*
7. *Give up your personal possessions*
8. *Sing to a live audience*
9. *Stay up all night*
10. *Take part in a protest*
11. *Cut your hair and donate it.*
12. *Be an extra in a film.*
13. *Write a blog.*
14. *Make a grand gesture*
15. *Face a fear.*
16. *See a psychic*

I read the list a few times. There are some already crossed out, of course, but most of the list is still to play for. I look at Marigold and she's staring at the page. She looks worried, as though the task is too big for her.

"It's a lot to do," she says.

"I suppose."

"And I have to do it now...you understand that, don't you? This...this is the only way I can move on. I've been thinking about this list since it happened....and I have to do it soon."

I blink. "But...what about us? If you go out to do the list...you'll be leaving us behind."

"You'll be okay here. Aunt Wilda can take better care of you for now than I can."

I don't understand. Rita is dead. Her priority now should be us, not the wishes of someone who will never be able to see her actions through. I think Rita never thought in a million years that she would die before we all grew up enough to look after ourselves. She wouldn't want Marigold leaving us behind for the sake of a bucket list. But I take one look at Marigold and know that she's right – she can't take care of us right now. She's barely taking care of herself. Maybe this is what she needs. Maybe she needs to get out of here for a while in order to heal. At least then, we'd have one mum back. If she can fix herself, then maybe she can put our family back together again.

Marigold takes my hand. "I'll still be around for a while. Only the volunteering will require me to travel. We can do some of it together! We can go through our things together, and sort out some stuff to go to the charity shop. And you can help me write my blog! We could write about something useful, something that can help people. Does that help at all?"

It does. It's like Marigold is reaching out to me for the first time since Rita died. It's like she wants me to share her pain and get through it together instead of hiding away from it all. For the first time in weeks, it doesn't feel like a solo race to recovery. I nod.

"I know what we need to do first. But I'll need some help."

I begin to clear the bed of clutter and Marigold watches me, her legs crossed on the bed. I chip a crust of paint from the bedsheet and then set Marigold's laptop on the duvet.

"We're going to stay up all night and watch movies. That's one thing off the list. But before we start, we're going to cut your hair. All of it."

Marigold lets out a half laugh, looking shocked. "Are you serious?"

"Yeah, I am."

"That's very spontaneous of you. Very out of character."

"It's being spontaneous on your behalf, it doesn't count."

"You're not actually going to be doing the hair cutting though, are you? You forget that I've seen your art homework. I'm not sure I trust you with cutting my hair…"

"Of course I won't cut it. We'll get Ro to do it. It's right up her street. She's been cutting her fringe since she could hold scissors."

Marigold laughs as I leave the room, and the noise takes me by complete surprise. It's a good surprise, though. I can't remember the last time she made such a happy sound. I'm smiling as I head for Ro's room. When I knock, I can hear her muttering moodily in her room and she throws the door open with a face like thunder. I lean against the doorframe, smiling.

"Hey. Fancy hacking off Marigold's hair and watching The Incredibles?"

Rowena narrows her eyes at me. "You've just appealed to my two favourite hobbies. I'm in. Where are the scissors?"

As she hunts them down, I head into my room and find Honey sprawled on her bed. She looks up at me with droopy eyes.

"I'm absolutely frazzled," she complains, stretching her skinny legs out.

"Would a massive bowl of microwave popcorn help?"

Honey's eyes sparkle with glee. "Absolutely."

"Go get some. We're all hanging out in Mari's room."

I feel like a kid at a sleepover, grabbing pillows and blankets to make the perfect film nest in Marigold's room. When I return, Rowena is tying Marigold's hair up while she bites her nails. She looks relieved to see me.

"How short are we going, boss?" Rowena asks me, a bobble in her mouth.

"It all has to go. There's got to be enough to donate. Once you've got rid of the length you can start to style the hair."

"Gotcha."

Marigold looks terrified. Rowena cackles, her scissors at the ready.

"It's only hair. It grows back."

"It'll take years to get back to the length it was…"

"So? You could do with a change in style, anyway. It's been long for as long as I've known you. Boooring."

Marigold cranes her neck to see herself in the mirror on the wall, fiddling with the ends of her hair. "I've been growing this since my hippie years."

"You mean these aren't your hippie years?"

Marigold grabs a sequined cushion and bashes Rowena with it, making her laugh.

"Don't wind me up. I'm the one with the scissors."

"That sounds more threatening than it should…"

Honey arrives on the scene with a huge bowl of popcorn, stuffing a few pieces in her mouth.

"What's going on?"

Marigold opens her arms. Rowena ducks beneath one and leans into her, while I take a place on the other side of her. "Family night. Films and fun. Rowena's going to cut my hair, so we can donate it to charity."

"Mum, that's so cool! But won't you feel a bit...a bit…"

"Naked?" Rowena says, snipping her scissors in the air. Marigold rolls her eyes.

"It'll be fine. Let's just get this over with."

Honey watches intently as Rowena prepares for her task. Even Ro looks nervous as the scissors fight to cut through the huge hunk of hair at the back of Marigold's head. I imagined it all falling gracefully in one go, but in reality, it takes almost a minute of Rowena hacking at it for it to come away. Marigold gasps as the weight falls away from her head. As Rowena ties the hair up securely, Mari's hands find her head, running over the short strands left behind. She looks like a different person – the hairstyle looks mature, but it makes her look younger. Maybe it's because her hair had become so limp, a chore for her to tend to. She smiles, stray hairs drifting like dandelion puffs from her head. Rowena pulls Mari's hands away from her head.

"Oi! I'm not done yet."

Marigold smiles, letting her hands fall to her side. "Sorry. Finish up, hairdresser."

Later on, when we're all tucked up watching a film, I look and see that Rowena and Honey have fallen asleep. Marigold is smiling at them fondly and she kisses the top of each of their heads. She reaches under the pillow for the list again and rests it on her knee. With a shaky hand, she crosses two items from her list. I rest my head against her shoulder and she kisses my forehead too. She slides the letter onto my knee.

"Just for now...let's keep this between us. Is that okay?"

I nod. I wouldn't want anything to spoil this moment right now. It's been a while since I can remember being this happy.

I don't want to lose that.

ALCOVE

The worst and only bad part of becoming a hermit is the boredom. Each day, I plough through my notes for each class, but I usually finish by one o'clock. I make lunch and eat it in front of the TV, but there's never anything good to watch during the day. I head back upstairs and twiddle my thumbs for a while, but I always end up back in the same place.

It was kind of a silent agreement between Honey and I that the alcove in our room belongs to me. She got the desk, I got my little reading nook. I've spent a little time decorating it so that it looks something straight from a Bookstagram feed. I draped my fairy lights carefully on the walls and added some colourful cushions to the wooden bench. This is the place that I retreat to when I've got nothing else to do, taking a book or my laptop with me, ready to spend another afternoon reading or writing.

I scan through my emails. Mrs Wickham sends me several a day, and she's set me all sorts of tasks. Her latest is one I'm trying to ignore – she wants me to post some of my work online.

I procrastinate for as long as I can. I make a sandwich. I take my time making hot chocolate and then convince myself I'll start work after I've finished drinking it. I click aimlessly through some of my favourite websites, but it only wastes ten minutes of my time. I sigh, checking the email again. Mrs Wickham recommended a website called Jotter, where young people share their stories and communicate with other readers and writers. I've never had an account on the site, but when I was still living with my parents, it got me through sleepless nights. I knew the password for my Dad's computer, and after they left the flat, I would log on and spend all night reading stories on the internet. It's a place I recognise, and it's a place that wouldn't be so awful to join. I sigh and click on the sign up button.

The website is colourful and bright with cute cartoons of stationery with googly eyes framing the screen. It looks a little childish to me now that I'm older, but the familiarity of it is nice. I look at the information the site is looking for. Name. Age. Email address. Username. I chew my thumb. I don't like the idea that anyone I know could stumble across the site and know I wrote the content here. There's a box to the side of the screen that reads:

Anonymity: If you wish to remain anonymous, feel free to use a pseudonym. It's always exciting to have a secret identity!

The prospect of going undercover makes me smile. I try to think of a name that would suit me – something that speaks something about me. I think of names of characters I've loved, or books that could inspire a nickname. My hands hover over the keys for a moment.

And then I think of it. I think of Vanessa and our love of *Chocolat*. I suddenly know exactly what my first name will be. It feels strange to write it in the name box, knowing it's a name that doesn't really belong to me. But for now, I'm borrowing it. I sit back, staring at the word.

Vianne. A French name, so elegant that it's hard to pair it with myself. But no one needs to know that the name doesn't suit me. Maybe a whole new identity can come with a whole new personality.

I fill out the rest of the form and excitement bubbles through me as the page loads, welcoming me to the site. I click through the site for a while, following some profiles – old familiar profiles and soon-to-be favourites. But my clicking takes me straight back to my own page, and I know it's time to upload something of my own.

There's one story I might be happy to post, but fear still consumes me as I open the document it's hidden in. It's the first story I showed to Rita, a few months ago before everything went wrong. I remember watching her read it. The way her face creased and her eyes crinkled as she laughed at the page in her hand. She had laid back on my bed, the page hovering above her face and a snort escaping as she laughed harder with each coming paragraph. And I knew it must have been good because Rita never lied – she would never laugh unless something tickled her.

I scroll through the page, reading it over one last time. Then, I highlight the whole thing and copy and paste it over. Quickly typing in a title, I sit back for a moment. This is it. I'm sending my work out into the world for anyone to see. The thought makes me nauseous. I take a moment to click through the site's other features to waste time. There's a button on the side instructing me to dedicate the story to someone. I smile. I type in her name. And then I click submit.

Rita's name sits atop my story when it's posted. It's surrounded by little pictures of rainbows and stars and suns. And I know it's the only place I want her to be right now.

I spend the rest of the day pretending that my online presence doesn't exist. I distract myself by writing something else so that I don't even have to think about it. But at five o'clock on the dot, I hear the ping of my laptop as I receive an email. I know it must be Mrs Wickham. I emailed her right after I posted my story so that she could read it over. I open the email and pray that she has something good to say.

The email isn't from Mrs Wickham directly. It's from Jotter, notifying me that I have a new comment. I assume she's made an account and left some notes. I open it and discover it's not from Mrs Wickham at all – someone I don't know has left their thoughts. I put my laptop down and move away from it. I don't want to look. They could have said anything. They could hate what I've written. What if I'm not funny? I've never thought I'm funny in real life. It's different on paper, when you have the time to think of how to be witty, how to make conversations flow, and how to make each end tie up neatly. In real life, I stutter and splutter incoherent answers. If I tried to tell a joke, I'd be there for hours trying to remember the punchline.

But I know I'll have to look eventually at what the person has said. I have to know what they think.

Even if it hurts me.

JOTTER

A newly published story by Vianne_Writes – the lesser known tale of the wolf in Little Red Riding Hood.

There's one golden rule for getting the finest meat possible in Wolferhampton: if it's under age twenty, we'll eat it plenty. But if it's getting old, it can't be sold.

If you're not from here, I suppose you're not familiar with the finest diner in town. It goes by the name of Kentucky Fried Children, better known to us locals as KFC. My brother Wulfric and his wife Lupita have been running it since I was a pup, and my Dad passed it on to Wulfy. I work there if I'm between jobs, wiping down tables and taking orders. This week, I've been working the nine till five shift. I was so busy serving earlier that I didn't have time to ask about all the frantic calls Lupita was making behind the counter. It's only now that I've finished that I can ask about it. Lupita and Wulfric call me over, their faces grave.

"We're in a spot of bother, Rudy," Wulfric admits, "Local produce is getting harder to come by. We seem to have exhausted our supply."

"Are you sure? All the kids are gone?"

"All the hunters keep coming back empty handed. There are barely any left."

"What about young adults? Surely they can't be gone too?"

Lupita shrugs. "We're a hungry bunch. It's all gone." She leans closer. "We've even been using over twenties," she whispers. I gasp and she hangs her head in shame.

"I know, Rudy, I know. We're going to have to start importing."

"Won't that be expensive?"

Wulfric nods, his eyes saddened as he scratches his snout. "Too expensive. We won't be able to keep it up for long. We need a miracle. Otherwise it looks like Kentucky Fried Children is going out of business."

"This can't be…we've been keeping this business going for generations. I refuse to let it go without a fight," I say. "Let's put our snouts together and think of some solutions."

We stand around talking until late in the night, but come up with nothing. In the end, they send me home and I walk through the forest with a heavy heart, paws trailing. KFC can't shut down. It's too important to us all. Wind claws through my fur, my head cast downwards. Preoccupied, I almost miss what's stuck to the tree nearby.

Almost.

There's a blur of crimson in the corner of my eye. I look up and see that it's a wrinkled poster stuck to the tree bark. I shuffle closer, heart thumping. I peel back the curled corner of the paper to see what it says.

Spring Costume Extravaganza. Lil Red feat DJ Gran. Wolferhampton Forest. Best Student Event of the Year!

I rub my paws together, my mouth salivating. Students! Under twenties! And if it's under age twenty, we'll eat it plenty! It looks as though we might have found our new source of protein…

There's a picture of a girl in a crimson hoodie, leaning over a DJ turntable. At the top of the picture, are the three words that make this opportunity truly perfect for getting KFC back on track.

Come in costume!

Our plan is simple.

Step 1: Crash the party.
Step 2: Party hard.
Step 3: Catch as much prey as possible.

Okay, so Wulfric says I should be concentrating on the important things (ie. Step 3), but I haven't been to a party in forever.

Of course, we all have our costumes set already. No skimpy witch costumes or zombie makeup for us. We'll be standing proud in our birthday suits. We just have to hope nobody notices what we really are.

The party is already in full flow when we arrive. The DJ set is actually pretty good. DJ Gran must be at least seventy, though. I shudder to think what she'd taste like. I bet she has dentures, and they're not easy to swallow, I tell you.

I've got my heart set on Lil Red, controlling the turntable in her crimson hoodie. I claimed dibs since this gig was my idea. And since she's the host, I reckon she'll be a good snack to keep me going for the rest of the hunt. I imagine she'd taste good southern fried with chips, but since I have a job to do, a blob of ketchup will have to do.

I'm looking for Lupita as I dance amongst the other students. When everyone's arrived, she's going to give the signal for us to strike. There are a lot of volunteers from the town – they can't resist a good hunt, and they want to keep KFC open as much as we do. But I'm starving. I didn't eat all day in preparation. I wish they'd hurry up.

The music suddenly screeches to a halt. Lil Red lowers her hood, grinning.

"I'm taking a short break! Need a quick drink..." She holds up a hip flask and I hoot along with the other rowdy teenagers. Getting into character can't hurt...

"Back in ten!" Red declares. She jumps down from the platform and DJ Gran takes centre stage. I catch Lupita's yellow eyes and she nods solemnly. It's time.

I smile.

I push my way out of the crowd, sneaking to the bar where I suspect Lil Red is residing. Sure enough, she's sat chatting to the barmaid as she pours her a cocktail. I'm tempted just to gobble her up, but she turns around, raising her glass in the air.

"Hi," she says, "Cool costume."

I feel my skin grow warm under my fur. "Oh! Thank you!"

"Come get a drink with me! Are you enjoying the set?"

"I sure am," I say, grinning toothily. But the party's barely started yet, in my eyes. I order a Bloody Mary (appropriate, I feel), but when I turn back to Lil Red, she's frowning at me.

"Man...your eyes are really yellow," she comments.

"Yeah, um...I got contacts."

"Oh. Well...you know that fur is pretty cool as well. Really shaggy. Authentic."

Excuse me? I comb my hair every day... "Yeah, well. I was going for that. Authentic."

"And are those...fleas?"

"Most certainly not!" I scowl. Preposterous! "How dare you!"

A glisten of spit lands on Lil Red's face. She looks disgusted as she wipes it away. There's a long silence as she smirks at me, looking me up and down.

"Dude, not to be rude, but I think you went a bit far with the costume. Your breath bloody stinks as well."

I sniff, throat tight. "You're so rude! I can't believe someone would say that..." This is not how this was supposed to go. Well, I'll show her. I can't wait any longer, snatching a bottle of sauce from the bar. I squirt a blob of ketchup straight on to Lil Red's shocked face. It should make me feel good, but her hurtful comments have gotten under my fur.

"I brush twice a day," I say miserably as I swallow her whole. I barely even taste her.

What a meanie.

I wash Lil Red down with my Bloody Mary and leave the barmaid a tip as she screams. She's not worth eating. She must be at least thirty-six. Practically ancient. She makes a run for it, screaming bloody murder, but she's not my concern anymore.

Let the hunt begin.

A strange quietness has settled in the forest. It's close to midnight and the volunteers are taking the fresh meat back to KFC in vans. It's been a good night for us. But something doesn't quite feel right. There's a chill resting on my spine. I'm surveying the area as wolves bustle past me with the meat. Normally, I'd be salivating at the thought of fresh game. But right now, I feel like I'm being watched.

I slip away to take a walk in the woods. My eyes dart from side to side, my ears pricking up at the slightest noise. Someone's following me. Suddenly, I hear a rustle of leaves behind me. I spin around. There, glasses perched on her nose, grey curls ruffled and gnarled hands holding an axe, is DJ Gran.

"You should've taken me down while you had the chance," she snarls. And with that, she slams the axe down on my tail. I howl, stumbling away and hopping around in agony. DJ Gran's axe is stuck in the ground, the remains of my tail jammed against the blade. Through blurred eyes, I watch her let the axe go and start to run. I snarl.

Evil Granny isn't going anywhere.

I know what I have to do. And it isn't pretty.

I hobble after her, pain blinding me. It's a good job she's slow. It doesn't take me too long to catch up.

She makes the mistake of looking back just as my mouth opens wide and snatches her up. I wince as I crunch down on her frail old bones and then swallow her withered body.

Dentures and all.

She leaves the taste of soap and wig hair in my mouth. Eckk. My stomach gurgles and I force myself to hold down my dinner. I collapse to the ground, stomach bulging, howling in pain. I can hear Wulfric calling my name, but I don't move. I'm feeling too sorry for myself. But at least I've learned something today.

If it's under age twenty, we'll eat it plenty. If it's getting old, it can't be sold. But no matter how mature, take them out, just to be sure.

Because Grannies bite back.

Be the first to like this post.

ProfessorVanessa commented: I like your style, Vianne. Keep it coming girl. V x

LIVING ROOM

I stare blankly at the computer, reading the comment over and over. *ProfessorVanessa*. It can't be a coincidence. Vanessa has somehow found my writing online.

The thought shouldn't terrify me this much, but it does. How do I know she actually likes it? She said she did, but she could easily just be laughing at me behind my back. Maybe she's sat at home right now, making fun of the home-schooled girl with all of her college friends. I put my head in my hands, pressing the heel of my hands into my eyes. My thoughts are toxic. Suddenly, I don't feel safe now, not even at home. My connections to the outside world have followed me into my safe space. I shudder. If I'm not safe here, where can I go?

I rush down the stairs and into the living room, closing the curtains. I shut the doors and turn the TV up so I can't even hear my own thoughts. Only then do I feel like I can breathe again.

What's wrong with me? Before today, I felt like everything was okay. As okay as it could be, anyway. But now I've given into my fears, and it's hard to claw myself out of it.

I decide I have to ask her. I won't be able to settle until I know. How am I supposed to approach this, though? I can't just ask her whether she likes me and my writing. I know how odd that would be. We barely know each other. It takes almost half an hour for me to construct a text that I can bear to send to her.

-ProfessorVanessa?

-Aye aye, Captain.

My heart stutters. Now what?

-How did you find me?

-I know you said you didn't want me to read your writing. But Mrs Wickham had us all upload on Jotter. I was clicking around when I found yours on the Recently Updated. I figured Vianne had to be you. I hope you don't mind.

I can't decipher her tone. Is she sympathetic, or a little cold? Each time I read it over it sounds different in my head. I wish I could hear her, or see her, but that's not an option. I take a deep breath and type.

-Was it okay? Did you like it?

I hit send and then realise that maybe it sounds like I'm fishing for compliments. I try to delete the text before it sends, but I'm too late. But she replies within seconds, and I'm spared the torture of waiting on her reply.

-Are you kidding? I loved it! So funny. You should have a little more confidence in yourself, Lori.

-Haha.

I sigh in relief. At least she says she was telling the truth. It's enough for now, but no doubt my scepticism will come flooding back. It always does. My phone buzzes again.

-Lori, I don't want to overstep here...but I get the feeling there's something you're holding back on. You never told me why you stopped coming to college. You don't have to tell me...I'm just curious. As a friend.

As a friend. She considers us friends. But how much do friends tell each other? I'm not entirely sure. I've never had many. For years, I was shipped around so often that at each new school, I didn't bother to even introduce myself. It was easier just to keep my head down until I moved again. That way I wasn't leaving anything good behind. I suppose Honey and Rowena count as friends, but they know my issues by default. They have to support me, as members of my family. Besides, Rowena is used to family drama. I suppose we all are, now. Now that Rita is gone.

I don't know how much she can handle. She seems like she comes from a normal family, with normal parents and normal issues. She has a dog that she walks every day. She goes to college, comes home, helps her father make dinner and they all sit and talk about their day. She does her homework, texts her friends and goes to bed at a sensible time.

That's not our family at all. We can't handle ourselves, let alone a dog. Our routines are so out of sync that sometimes members of the household go days without seeing each other. At bedtime, Honey studies by lamplight until all hours of the morning. Rowena can't sleep for nightmares and at 3am, I hear her go downstairs to make black coffee. Marigold spends more of the day asleep than the night. Who knows what Wilda does, because really, I barely know her at all. From outside, Wilda's home looks like any other on the street – a neatly trimmed house with perfection behind its walls. We're not perfect, and that's okay for us. I'm just not sure what other people would make of us.

I begin to type, barely thinking as I let my emotions spill out.

-There's a reason I don't go to college. There's a reason why every time you ring I watch my phone without answering, praying you won't call a second time. There's a reason you won't see me walking down the road any time soon, or coming to Rococo's with you. I don't ever leave here. I don't ever want to leave again. I'm scared of everything beyond my doorstep. I've only known bad things to happen to me out there. I don't feel safe anymore. And if that sounds crazy, it probably is. But I can't help it, and that's how it is.

I send my ramble before I can change my mind. And then it's a waiting game. I don't expect to wait long. Vanessa is a fast texter. But minutes stretch on. Ten. Then fifteen. I chew my thumb. I start to think she's not going to reply again. I fumble out another message.

-I understand if you never speak to me again.

I hope she at least replies to let me know she's done with me. Silence is the worst thing I could have hoped for. But I realise as I wait that it's worse than that – if she never speaks to me again, I've lost the first chance I've had at a friend in years. And right now, I feel like it could tip me over the edge.

There's a knock on the door, but I can't bear to open it. Not in the state I'm in. But the knock comes again, and I know that if I don't answer it, Marigold will. And then I'll have to face another lecture about therapy and how low I'm getting. I don't want that. As I stand to go to the door, I get a text.

-I'm outside.

My legs won't move. She's probably here to tell me she never wants to see me again. I wish I could shake myself and tell myself to get it over and done with. I hear Vanessa call out to me. And suddenly I'm standing by the door. My hand is on the handle. The door opens.

Vanessa is standing with two takeout cups in her hands. Her usual beam is replaced with a soft smile. I know that face. It's a face of sympathy. She holds out a cup to me, simultaneously taking in my pyjamas, my messy hair and my tear stained face.

"I know you can't go to Rococo's so…I thought I would bring Rococo's to you."

I try to smile, but the gesture just sets me off crying again. Vanessa looks worried, placing the cups on the window ledge and rushing forwards to hug me. Her arms feel strange around me. I can't decide if it's comforting or something else entirely. But I let her hold me because pushing her away right now is the last thing I want to do. This might be the last chance to salvage what we've built.

I try my best not to cry too much. I let myself whimper for a few moments and then I pull away. I wipe my eyes and laugh shakily. Vanessa picks up one of the cups and extends it out to me. I don't know what else to say or do, so I just sip the hot chocolate. The warmth trickles through my body and makes me shiver. Vanessa's smile grows a little.

"Good, right?"

I nod, averting my eyes back to the cup. "So good."

"Shall we sit down?"

I nod and show her through to the living room. She sinks into the sofa, kicking her shoes off and curling her feet under her. It's strange to see that she feels more at home here than I'm ever likely to. I perch on the end of the sofa, sipping more hot chocolate so that I don't have to speak.

"Do you want to talk?"

I do, but right now, I'm drained. I don't have the energy for a conversation with so much weight. I feel like I might fall, even though I'm sitting down. Vanessa nods at my silence, understanding. She fishes in her bag.

"It's okay. I have an antidote for you."

I watch as she moves to the television, a disc in her hand. She slots it into the ancient DVD player and I watch as familiar images appear on the startup screen. Vianne's cheeky smile, a chocolate propped between her fingers as she eyes up Roux. Vanessa smiles at me.

"Will this help?"

I stare at her. The first person since Rita to act like my panic attack didn't even take place. The first person since who has known exactly what to do. No awkward silences or trying not to address the elephant in the room. Somehow, Vanessa gets what my family never will – that all I need right now is to feel normal.

"I think it could do."

She grins and presses play, skipping back to the couch, her knees drawn to her chest and her cup of hot chocolate in her hand. Then we lapse into silence so we can lose ourselves in a world more magical than our own.

KITCHEN

Saturday mornings in Wilda's house are usually pretty crazy. It's the only day when everyone is at home all day, and after the quietness during the week, it feels almost like a completely different place. Rowena spends half the time running around and causing trouble, leaving a mess behind her like a mini hurricane. Honey sees Saturdays as her 'relaxing' days. What she means by that is that she takes over the entire living room, the TV quietly chattering away in the background while she studies, her books spread over every surface and bowls of snacks wedged between her knees. Even Marigold seems to come alive, sometimes taking her equipment out on the patio where she paints in her pyjamas, a glass of wine in her hand that makes her giggles return if even for a moment.

But today, it's quiet. October is in full swing, and with it the promise of Halloween lurks, getting the kids on the street in the mood for autumnal fun. They're wrapped up in scarves their mothers made them wear, and they waddle past the house in puffed out coats.

Inside our house, though, it's never been quieter. Honey has gone out to visit some friends – a rare outgoing moment in her inactive social life – and Rowena hasn't left her room as of yet. I checked on Marigold earlier, only to find her tucked up in bed, reading over Rita's list. I sensed she wanted to be alone and left her to her own devices. With Wilda out at the store, it feels like any other day of the week – quiet and lonely and monotonous.

So I opt to spend my day in the kitchen. I take my time making myself a fry up. Rita didn't often allow us to eat something so indulgent, dubbing it a treat, and I never minded. But lately, food is one of the things that keeps my moods in check. Cooking gives me something to do, something to distract me, and then the reward is always a meal that makes my mouth water. I've noticed since being here that I've started to fill out a little, my previously flat stomach now pushing against my jeans. But it feels good. While my mental health is pretty bad, my body feels nourished and cared for. Gaining weight isn't a concern for me. In fact, I think it might be a good thing. It feels like I'm healing.

The food is starting to smell pretty incredible. I plate it up and sit by myself at the small kitchen table. I get the sense that this is where Wilda used to dine before we arrived. It certainly looks more used than the dining table, and it only really seats two people. Some people don't like to eat alone, but I prefer it. It feels therapeutic in some ways, not having to think about the others who would usually be at the table. Especially recently, dinners have been tense, with one person or another butting heads. This feels good to me.

I've just about finished eating when I hear a loud bang at the door, making me spill my water on myself. I curse, trying to dry myself off with a tea towel. I assume it'll be Wilda returning, needing a hand with the shopping. I head to the door, but a key is already turning in the lock. Before I can reach for the handle, the door flies open and Vanessa flounces in. She's not her usual self – that much is evident straight away. She's wearing what looks like a nightie with embroidered teddy bears, and a pair of fluffy slippers with googly eyes. Her hair is limp around her face and her cheeks are flushed. She throws her hands in the air when she spots me.

"I'm an idiot! A complete idiot! A hundred fairy cakes I promised. One bloody hundred! Who has time to make one hundred cakes? And instead of starting yesterday like I should have done, I completely forgot about it. I faffed around getting my nails done at the salon, and now I'm definitely going to chip them. Unless you have an electric mixer, but even then, these nails aren't made to withstand a full day of baking. RIP, nails."

Perplexed, I watch her dive into the kitchen and shuffle after her. Vanessa's kneeling on the counter, scouting out the cupboards. She pulls out a bag of flour. It's slightly open at the top, and her hair is suddenly sprinkled in white powder. She sneezes boisterously, her face buried in her arm.

"Well, none of this is going well."

"...don't take this the wrong way, but have you finally gone completely insane?"

Vanessa cracks a laugh, hopping down from the counter. "I should have explained. I volunteered to help with a charity fair at my old primary school. I promised to have a cake stall, and they wanted a hundred cakes from me. I thought it was a little excessive, but apparently there's a lot of demand for cake at these things."

"I can imagine."

"Can you bake? Two hands are better than one. Wait, no. Four hands! Well, technically still two if you agree to help because to be honest I'm useless at baking and this was a horrible idea."

I blink, taking it all in. She speaks so fast sometimes that it takes my brain a moment to catch up. After a delayed reaction, I laugh. "Don't worry. We'll get this under control. I know some recipes."

"Oh thank God, you're a saviour. So, what's the plan, boss? What flavour are we making? What do we need?"

"I've got a book somewhere. We can look for some inspiration."

I run upstairs to find my baking manual and head back downstairs, waving it triumphantly at Vanessa. She takes it from me and opens it eagerly, flipping the pages in a frenzy. She stops when she spots a picture of chocolate frosted cupcakes. She looks at me for my approval and I shrug.

"Everyone likes chocolate, right?"

"Right. And I don't want to sell to people who don't."

"Not even for charity?"

"Not even. You can't trust someone who doesn't like the sweeter things in life, Lori."

I can't help smiling as she heads to the fridge, consulting the recipe for the ingredients needed. I help her out, ransacking the cupboards for the basics. It doesn't take us long to figure out that we've only scrounged enough for two batches of twelve cakes. I write a list of the things that we need then send Vanessa to the shop, lending her some clothes suitable to leave the house in. Then I get to work.

The recipe is easy enough to follow. I used to bake with Rita sometimes, but I usually let her do most of the work. I used to like helping her out, but mostly, it was an excuse to spend more time with her. Plus, it meant eating cake straight out of the oven. Nothing is better than something baked fresh. I love the smell of it all, and the warmth it leaves inside you when you eat something straight from the oven. I smile to myself. It's the simple pleasures, sometimes.

I hear Wilda come in with her shopping, the bags rustling as she waddles through to the kitchen. She's surprised to see me, whisk in hand and the oven humming behind me as it heats up.

"You're baking?"

"Yeah. Vanessa has a thing. I said I'd help her out."

Wilda doesn't say anything, but when I look over, she's smiling, piling groceries into the fridge. "If I'd known, I could have got your ingredients."

"It's okay. Vanessa and I have gone halves."

"That's nice. You two seem to be getting along well."

I nod without looking up, washing my batter covered hands under the hot tap. I suspect they'll be dirty again in minutes, but the goop on my hands is pretty unappealing. "Yeah. She's really nice."

"It's good that you've made a friend. I approve. She's a sweet girl."

There's something strange about her tone. It takes me a moment to put my finger on what it is. She's referring to Vanessa as though she's my crush. I frown, looking up to see if Wilda is watching me, but she's got her back to me, packing the last of the shopping away.

But she's already made her point – she's letting me know that she knows. She knows I like girls.

I wonder how on earth she figured it out. It's not like I give any indicators that I know of. Rita once told me it's my reaction to watching TV. Honey is always swooning over men in programmes. Before she became obsessed with studying, she went through a phase of binge watching Teen Wolf every night. She'd comment on the shirtless guys and curse that her dream guy lived in the fictional Beacon Hills. Sometimes, she would write fanfiction just to spend more time in her mind with her imaginary lover. She'd ask my opinion and I'd stare at the tanned, bare chests of the main characters, wondering what the appeal was. I'd just shrug and tell her she could have them.

It was only when we started watching costume dramas that Rita figured it out. I had a habit of commenting on the beauty of the women, with their large crinoline dresses and elaborate hairstyles that none of us could hope to replicate ourselves. I never ogled the women in the shows in the same way Honey did to the men. That was something Rita commented on - she told me that I reacted differently to someone if I liked them. It was something she'd recognised in herself – the exercising of caution about what we say and how we say it. Straight girls don't have to worry about being too overtly heterosexual, while queer people are always wondering how they'll be perceived by others. It's a sad fact. But it was all these little clues that led Rita to realise my feelings before I ever admitted them out loud.

Of course, by that point, I'd figured it out for myself, so I didn't mind Rita asking me about it. It didn't come as a shock to me. But after that, I was always a little more careful about what I said. I wasn't ashamed in any way, but I knew that Honey and Rowena couldn't relate to me in that sense – it always felt easier to stay quiet about it. And it's the same now - it's not like I keep my feelings a secret. It's just strange to think that my aunt, who I've only known for a short time, figured it out quicker than Marigold did. Rita was a lot quicker to the mark, of course. She was intuitive like that.

I absent-mindedly move to put the first cakes in the oven, very aware that Wilda is in the room. It must be another skill that Rita and Wilda share. I wish I could read her mind right now. Is she laughing at me – a girl so closed off about her feelings being as easy to read as an open book? Maybe. But at least if she's laughing, then I'm in on the joke. I get the feeling she'd never laugh *at* me. It's not in her nature.

I start on the next batch of cakes, but something is plaguing me – it's almost as though Wilda has brought to my attention how much I actually do like Vanessa. I've spent so much time being nervous around her that I've forgotten the signs of liking someone – the flutters in your stomach, laughing at everything they say, wondering what they're doing when you're apart. But it's more than that too. I scour the internet to find things I think might make her smile. I've re-read Chocolat twice since we've met so that I can send her quotes from the book. We discovered last week that there's a sequel we'd miraculously never heard of and I bought us both a copy the very next day, handing it to her covered in pink tissue paper that I thought she'd find cute. We spent that evening sitting on our window sills on opposite sides of the street, waving to each other occasionally as we read it in unison. It has felt so good to have a friend to share everything with that I might have forgotten that there's a thin line between friendship and love, and I'm definitely toeing it.

The front door slams and I jump out of my thoughts. She's back. The thought makes me blush. And there's another sign, each new one taking me by surprise. She rattles her bag in excitement, and then pulls a face as something clatters in the bag.

"Oops. Could be the eggs. I hope none are broken. Hey Wilda!"

The pair of them hug and I pretend to keep myself busy, stirring the already thoroughly combined mix. Vanessa comes up behind me and hugs me tight.

"Thanks again for being such a gem. I'd never get this done on my own."

I catch Wilda's eye and she looks smug as she leaves the room. I shiver. I can imagine Rita reacting in exactly the same way. For a second, it's almost like she's in the room with me.

Vanessa brushes past me, breaking me out of my thoughts. She crouches by the oven to look inside.

"It smells so good in here. You've finished the first lot already?"

"Not yet. They need to be cooled for a while, and then iced. And then there's another seven batches of twelve cakes to go."

Vanessa puffs, her hands on her hips. "Well blimey. This could take all bloody day."

I'm starting to hope so. An entire day with her feels like a privilege I'm not sure I deserve. Vanessa produces her phone and props it on the windowsill, pressing shuffle on a playlist on her music app.

"Let's get down to business," she declares. As a dramatic show tune blares through the kitchen, she grabs the bowl from my hand and stirs it dramatically, waltzing around the room as she does. I snort and roll my eyes. I can already tell she's not going to be much help. She belts out showtunes, one after the other while I make more mixture. She seems to take on the role of keeping an eye on the cakes. After she fills each case, she sits cross legged in front of the oven, watching carefully and humming. Wilda swoops into the kitchen a few hours in and ruffles Vanessa's hair.

"A watched pot never boils, dear."

"Ahh, but this is no pot, Wilda. This is cake. A completely different thing."

Wilda stands next to me. The fully ready cakes sit on the sideboard, neatly arranged in a row.

"Can I have one?"

"No!" Vanessa and I cry in unison. Wilda chuckles, shaking her head.

"Alright, alright. Next time, keep a batch aside for me."

"We can make a big one for your birthday. Or for Halloween! What do you reckon, Lori?"

I raise an eyebrow. "Are you sure you can handle doing this again so soon?"

"Sure I can. You're the one doing all of the work."

I flick flour at Vanessa and she laughs as it speckles her cheeks. Wilda tuts and rolls her eyes with an affectionate smile.

"Make sure you clean up this mess later, girls," she says, but she doesn't sound too bothered. I think she's just glad to see me smiling. How strange it must be for her, living in a house with all these new people who walk around like they're haunted by ghosts. Now, perhaps we look as though we have returned to the land of the living, even if only for a while.

The baking doesn't stop, but we start losing momentum around four o'clock, when Vanessa's playlist comes to a harrowing close with a song from Phantom of the Opera. The silence it brings makes me nervous at first, but I don't have the energy for conversation. That's why it's a relief when at five o'clock, Wilda returns with a pizza box in her hand, steam coming out the sides of the box.

"One piping hot pepperoni pizza for the bakers."

It feels weird to eat pizza after my birthday. I haven't touched the stuff since. But when the box opens, revealing cheese spilling from the sides of the bread and crisp pepperoni layers on top, my stomach growls. I know if Rita could see me, she'd shove a slice in my hand and tell me to enjoy it, the way we did together so many times. I wonder if Wilda knows the finer details of that night. I think she must. And maybe she's stepping into Rita's shoes again, trying to give me a sign that for now, everything's okay.

Wilda leaves me with Vanessa and we sit on the floor, eating pizza. Vanessa's face lights up as she takes her first bite.

"This is exactly what I needed. My mum's very strict about junk food. She doesn't let us have it very often. Only on special occasions. But sometimes, nothing will do but a greasy takeout pizza."

I nod in agreement as I battle with a stringy piece of cheese. "Our family has always been the same. But you're right. Sometimes, this is exactly what is needed."

"I feel bad now, when my parents are so good in the kitchen. The magic they whip up together is incredible. They like to do themed weeks, where they cook food from different countries each time. It's Italian week, so I guess takeout pizza kind of counts."

"What's their speciality?"

"My mum likes to make Polish food, since her grandmother was Polish. I think it's nice that she reminds us of our family history. She makes really great *pierogi,* and she's obsessed with 'putting on a spread' so she tends to just make lots of side dishes so people can pick and choose what they like to eat. My parents love making a fuss and having guests over. Wilda has been a few times to test out the goods. I wish that you could come too, some day. Or hey, maybe we should bring the party over here. Wilda is going to be sick of the sight of me."

"I don't see how that would be possible," I say with a smile. Vanessa grins back.

"I'm not to everyone's taste. I'm kind of loud and full-on, in case you hadn't noticed."

I laugh. "I think I might have noticed just a little…it doesn't bother you? What people think of you?"

Vanessa scoffs. "Not at all. I can't control it. I can maybe change people's minds about me, but I'm not going out of my way to make people feel comfortable in my presence. I'm a nice person. I'm not hurting anyone. If someone has a problem with me, then that's their business."

"I wish I was like that."

Vanessa smiles softly. "It's all about letting go. I used to get caught up in things a lot more. But I think life gets easier when you accept that you can't control everything. I know that's easier said than done…but for me, it gives me peace of mind."

"I guess I'm the opposite. I don't like anything I can't control in some way. It scares me. Is that stupid?"

"No," Vanessa says gently. "It isn't. It's probably sensible. Sensibility has never been my thing."

I smile. I know she's only trying to make me feel better, but it's worked a little. I think she senses that one of her tangents would come in handy now, because she clears her throat with a grin.

"Anyway, yeah. Everyone in my family is a cook. Except for me, so far. I think instead I inherited my grandmother's writing skills. Nothing wrong with that, I suppose."

"Your parents will train you up in the kitchen yet."

Vanessa laughs. "They can dream. I do like to help them in the kitchen sometimes, but their cooking is much better than anything I could ever make. They put time and effort in, you know? The way we would for writing. Hours learning recipes. Hours figuring out the best places to buy fresh herbs for the best prices. They must have put years into perfecting some of their dishes. It's the kind of stuff that has you desperate for second helpings, even when your stomach is bulging and you've had to undo the buttons on your jeans."

I smile, nibbling a piece of pepperoni. "I love that feeling. They sound passionate. Your family is so interesting."

Vanessa smiles. "I could talk all day about them. To be honest, I could talk all day, full stop."

"I get that feeling."

She shoves me playfully and I topple backwards, laughing. Vanessa takes my hand to pull me upright and I treasure the few seconds where our hands interlink, wishing she'd keep her grip in mine. She doesn't, but a girl can dream.

"Don't you think the best part of a new friendship is just...getting to know each other?" she says, mutilating her pizza by pulling off bits of cheese. "I just love finding out what makes people tick. But I've gotta say...you take your time. Opening up, I mean. I feel like I hog the limelight."

She does, of course, but how could she not? I can't be the only person who sits and watches her in awe, happy just to lap up her every word for hours on end.

"It's okay. I like to listen."

"But so do I. I know I don't seem like I do...I've just got a lot to say. It all kind of comes tumbling out, you know? I feel like I don't give you a chance to speak."

I smile, dipping my head so she can't see me blush. "It's okay. We've got time."

She grins. "Yeah. All the time in the world."

When we're too full to finish the pizza, we leave it to go cold and return to baking. When we reach the last batch of cakes, the kitchen is a bombsite; egg yolk smeared on the worktops, a dust cloud of icing sugar and flour hanging in the air and on my clothes. A collection of ingredients are gathered on top of the microwave, a mountain of used bowls and spoons piled in the sink. The low buzz of the mixer fills the air as we wearily make the last batter. Despite Vanessa's fear of breaking her nails, now she seems to be up to her elbows in cake mix. She grabs the whisk and dips it back in the bowl, letting the mixer create a hurricane of raw batter. Before she carries on, she tilts the bowl for me to inspect. I dip my spoon into the bowl to check it out.

The runny ingredients have combined beautifully, my spoon swirling through the golden-yellow batter gracefully. It's ready to go in the cases; pink paper cups awaiting the cake mix. We haphazardly scoop large helpings of the batter. At the start, it was a process of precision, when we allowed it to drizzle slowly into a cake case, watching it nestle in the grooves of the paper without making a mess up the sides. Now, as long as there's batter being transferred, we don't care. A whole day of baking is enough to tire anyone out.

When all the cases are filled, I slide the tray in the oven and wait, my mouth watering. We talk a little, but we're distracted. Our eyes are on the oven almost constantly, watching our cakes bloom. Impatiently, we open the oven door, prodding half-baked cakes and coming away with warm gloop on our fingertips.

We force ourselves to wait.

The room is filled with the smell of baking and burned sugar from the third batch that didn't turn out so well. We sit close together on the floor, leaning back on our hands to support our tired bodies. Our hands are nearly touching. I want to close the gap, but I can't judge how risky a move it is. Instead, I let the anxiety of whether to move or not consume me until our timer finally gives a tinny chime. The cakes are ready. Warmth hits my face as I take them out of the oven. We set them on the side, our icing ready to be piped. Now all we can do is wait.

Vanessa's lips move quietly as she counts the cakes, muttering numbers like she's doing roll call. She smiles, catching my eye.

"We've made it. A hundred cakes. Plus four spare." She picks up one of the wonkier cakes from the latest batch, still warm from the oven. She smears chocolate frosting on it, and it immediately seems to collapse, melted by the heat of the cake. A dip into the bowl of sugar strands and the cake is a lopsided version of perfect. She unfolds the pink casing, folding it flat so it looks like a Japanese parasol lying on her palm. Then she holds the cake out to me, her fingers coated in chocolate icing as it drips.

We lean in at the same time to take a bite.

There's chocolate icing on my chin. The cake crumbles slowly in my mouth. Then the cool, rich icing slides across my tongue and the crunch of the sugar sprinkles shocks my system. The snack feels forbidden. I know Vanessa feels the same when she bares her teeth devilishly, chocolate coating her teeth.

"If my dentist could see me now…" she whispers. I loll my tongue, trying to reach the icing on my chin. It earns a laugh from Vanessa. She throws her head back when she laughs the hardest. It's cute. Really cute. The icing continues to melt, dribbling up her arm. She watches the situation get worse and worse.

"There's no saving this situation, is there?"

"Nope."

"What happened in here?"

We turn and see Wilda and Marigold standing in the doorway. Vanessa and I look at one another and burst out laughing. They look bewildered for a moment, but then I think I see Marigold crack a smile. It might be the first time she's seen me laugh so freely in over a month, and to her, that can only mean one thing.

Progress.

CYBERSPACE

The internet has always fascinated me. It's like the universe – there's no end to it. It's always expanding. There's more information there than any human could ever process in a lifetime. And yet, somehow, so many people have stumbled across my little corner of the internet where I've been hiding out.

I'm reading through my latest comments on my story on Jotter. They've been rolling in faster this week, with a few people a day discovering it. It's made it into the site's ranking of popular retellings. It's exciting, to say the least. For the first time, I feel confident in my abilities. I check the site every few hours and almost always find new comments left for me. I'm looking through them when Honey gets home, entering our bedroom and dumping her bag with a flourish. She retreats immediately to her bed, puffing as her head hits the pillow.

"What a day."

"Everything okay?" I ask. Honey hasn't been around much as of late. She's been going out more and more with her new friends, but of course, being Honey, it's usually for study groups. She missed dinner this evening for a study group near college. I assume one of her friends brought her home.

"I'm just tired," Honey says. She reaches into her bag and pulls out a sheet of pills. She pops two from the wrapper and swallows them dry.

"What's that?"

"Just paracetamol," she says dismissively. "What's that you're looking at there?"

I show her the screen. She scans it with a small smile.

"There are nearly a hundred comments…"

"And that's just for this story. Some of my other ones have got loads of attention."

"I thought you weren't too keen on posting online?"

I shrug. "I wasn't at first. I didn't like the idea of putting myself out there. But now I think it's kind of great. Mrs Wickham proofreads things before I post so I don't have to be scared of making some stupid grammar mistake or anything. Vanessa reads everything I post too. She always leaves the sweetest comments."

"I bet she does," Honey says with a smile sweet as sugar, but there's a teasing undertone to her comment. Before I can ask what she's implying, she cuts in again. "I think it's great. It's good for you."

I smile, watching her click through some of my stories. Her smile seems to get bigger as she goes through each one. Then she closes my laptop lid.

"At Christmas, I swear I'm going to sit down with a brew and read every single one." She pats the bed beside her and I eagerly take up the spot. It's been a long time since Honey and I sat side by side and chatted. Honey watches me for a moment before pulling me in for a long hug. I'm a little surprised, but I don't mind. It's nice for her to be her old affectionate self again. Her chin digs into my shoulder.

"I don't say it enough, but I'm proud of you. I know it's been tough. Honestly, I've had a hard time keeping it together. I should have been a better sister and looked after you. But I just-"

"Don't, Honey. It's fine. Besides…we should be looking after each other." I pull away and see that Honey's face is stained with tears. I panic. I don't think I've ever seen Honey cry. She's a very private person. Anyone who doesn't know her might think that she's just happy all the time, but I think she's just good at looking like she's fine when she isn't. She doesn't like people seeing her like this, red faced and blotchy. I grab a tissue from our bedside table and hand it to her. She tries to laugh to mask the tears, but it makes her worse and her face crumples. But when I reach to pull her in again, she fans me away, sniffing.

"It's okay. Don't. I just need a minute."

It's hard watching her push me away, but there's not a lot I can do. I sit back and watch as she pulls herself together. I hear her muttering to herself under her breath, encouraging herself, telling herself that she's fine And somehow, she convinces herself. When she looks up, her eyes are clear, her lips pressed together.

"Ignore me. I'm being silly."

"But-"

"Honestly, I'm fine! I'm going to grab some leftovers from dinner, okay?" she says. I watch her stumble to her feet and head out of the room as quickly as she can. I want to go after her, but bringing up the incident would just embarrass her. I know that well enough because I've been there. After a panic attack, the worst thing anyone can do is keep bringing it up. Marigold used to do it – she'd treat me like a baby, asking if I wanted something sweet or a mug of hot milk. Rita eventually told her to stop, but I remember it upsetting me at the time.

There's a ping on my computer. I don't recognise the noise – it's not the same as any of my other notifications. I open the laptop and see that I have a message on Jotter. The sight of it makes my heart seize. I've not had any private messages before. Comments are fine – they're impersonal, not directed to the author, but rather to the story. I often reply to comments, but it's not an act that leads to the pressure of conversation. Private messages are different. There are so many potholes. Do you ask questions to get the conversation rolling, or let a dry conversation come to a dead end? Can you get away with sarcasm, or does it lead to people reading the message wrong and getting offended? How many emojis is too many emojis? Is a wink face a sign of flirtation (I learned the hard way that it is.) To me, online conversation is just wrong. I've always argued that humans aren't meant to be in contact twenty-four seven; we weren't born with the internet served to us on a platter. Once upon a time, people used to have to actually speak to one another face to face, and even then it wasn't all the time. Still, I'm stuck in this world, not that one, and I've never been good at face to face conversation anyway, so now I guess it's time to face the fact that there's a message waiting for me in my inbox.

I click on the message. It's punctuated with smiley faces and overly friendly symbols for someone I've never spoken to before.

xsweetxdreamsx: *Hi Vianne! I've been reading your stories, and I love them! You've got such a great writer's voice. I wondered if you'd like to chat? I always like to make friends on Jotter!*

How am I supposed to reply to that without sounding like an idiot? First I'll have to thank her and gush about how nice she is so that she doesn't think I'm rude. Then it's not like I can tell her that, actually, I don't want to chat – I don't know this person, I feel like it would be awkward. But then I remind myself that I'm not replying as Lori – I'm replying as Vianne, and she is whoever I want her to be. I think of the traits I crave. The ones that girls like Vanessa ooze; charming, charismatic, funny, confident. I decide Vianne is all of those things. After all, she's just another character – except she's taking on my story.

Vianne_Writes: *Hi xsweetxdreamsx. Thanks so much for reading – it's made my day knowing you enjoy my stories. Sure! I love to chat too.*

It feels like an awkward place to leave the message, but I can't think of anything else to add. I press send and immediately feel sick. I feel like it was such a boring, generic answer, that the girl won't even bother to respond again. But minutes later, my laptop pings again. I pull my laptop onto my lap, curious at her reply.

xsweetxdreamsx: *You're very welcome! I look forward to more of your stories. Let's go with an icebreaker, shall we? Tell me your favourite novel and why.*

It's a good question, and one I'm more than comfortable with answering. But what would Vianne reply? I decide that it's perfectly acceptable that she'd say the book from which she got her name.

Vianne_Writes: *I love the novel, Chocolat. It's just magical and enchanting and, well, what's not to love about a book centering around chocolate? I actually stole my Jotter name from the book. My name isn't really Vianne, but I wanted to remain anonymous. It hasn't even worked, really, but that was the reason behind it.*

xsweetxdreamsx*: That's alright. Me too. Most people call me Dream. Just because of my username. It sounds like a great book. You can never have enough chocolate in your life, after all…have you read Birdsong? I have such an interest in history, and I know it's not about that, but it really transported me. I felt like I was really there. Have you ever felt that?*

It's like speaking to my clone. Someone with exactly the same interests as me – history, reading, chocolate…okay, maybe a lot of people like those things. But it feels okay. This is someone I could feel comfortable talking to. Especially when they have no idea who I am, what I look like. If it all goes wrong, there's nothing lost. I'm smiling as I type.

Vianne_Writes: *I know exactly what you mean. I could talk about books for hours.*

xsweetxdreamsx: *Shall we?*

I smile. I think my day is about to get much better.

I wake to a new message from Dream. I was up late last night talking to her, long after Honey had given up on her homework and gone to bed. I dreamt of Jotter all night, the way you do after playing several hours of Tetris. The cartoon icons from the site swam around messages from Dream in my mind. We talked about everything under the sun; books and history and school and friendship and family. I would have been happy to stay up all night talking, but my body disagreed and drifted off at some point. But the moment I woke up, Honey was already gone and I felt no issue in reaching straight for my laptop to check my messages.

xsweetxdreamsx: *Ha, so true! It must be pretty late for you over there so I'm guessing you've gone to bed. It says you're offline. Talk soon!*

That's the worst response I could have hoped for. The conversation has come to an end. Now it feels like I have to come up with something interesting to kick start us again. I bite my lip. It takes me a while, but eventually I come up with something that I think might be alright.

Vianne_Writes: *I practically fell asleep at my laptop. I'm not used to late nights! I just wondered....you know the origin of Vianne_Writes. What made you choose xsweetdreamsx? I'm always curious about people's usernames. They all seem very random to me, but I'm sure everyone has their origin stories. How did you come up with yours?*

I get on with my day, knowing it must be an inconvenient time for her since she's offline. It's only when Honey and Rowena get home that I check my messages again. I'm delighted to find she's replied.

xsweetxdreamsx: *It's not random. It's actually kind of a sad story.*

Her response wasn't exactly what I imagined. I chew my lip as I reply.

Vianne_Writes: *You don't have to tell me.*

xsweetxdreamsx: *It might be quite nice to tell someone, actually. You're the only person who has ever asked.*

Vianne_Writes: *Well, I'm all ears if you want to talk about it.*

She takes a long time replying, and I think at first she's decided against the whole idea. It would make sense. But then a long paragraph comes through. I almost don't want to read it, but I'm too curious not to.

xsweetxdreamsx: *My Mom was in the army. She met my Dad when she was on leave in San Diego and they fell in love. They traded letters for years, always seeing each other during Mom's time away from the army. But she was dedicated to serving her country, and he's always been super focussed on his career. Dad always said he didn't mind the distance so much because it was always worth the wait when Mom came home. They got married and had their honeymoon, then she inevitably went back to fight. Imagine his surprise when she came home early from tour, having discovered she was three months pregnant.*

I smile. The story kind of sounds like a modern-day fairy tale. I wish the story would end there, but I get the feeling it's about to take a turn for the worse. I wait while she types, imagining a girl in LA, looking out the window at the bright lights and the midnight sky, wondering how the hell to tell a complete stranger her life story.

xsweetxdreamsx: *She stayed at home until I was five. She was a good Mom. She used to take me to school, to karate, make healthy dinners for me so that I got strong. Dad was always great too. They were a good duo. And then Mom decided that she had to go back to the army a few years after 9/11 happened. I like to think I remember the day when she left, but I don't think I do. I think I remember what my Dad has told me more than anything.*

xsweetxdreamsx: *Mom wrote to us. She did call sometimes, but I liked her letters. I could keep them, and hold on to them the way I couldn't hold on to her voice after she called. I still have all the letters. Hundreds of them. Sometimes when I miss her, I get them out and read them. Dad used to read them to me when I was very little, but when I learned to read and write, I used to spend my Monday evenings replying to the letters that had come that morning. I would tell her every mundane detail of my life – what I ate for breakfast, what games I played at lunchtime, and what cartoons Dad and I watched in the evenings, because Dad said she'd want to know. Her replies were shorter than my letters, but full of love. She never told me much about what she was doing, but she'd tell me she missed me, and sign each letter off with a poem. Her spare time was for poetry, and I came to know that and admire her for it. I wanted to be just like her. A poet, a soldier, a hero.*

xsweetxdreamsx: *I missed her a lot, but like my Dad said; it made it that much better when she came home. But one time she didn't come home. We got a letter in the post, but it wasn't from her. Dad started crying a lot. And when he told my Mom was* *coming home, but to be buried, our whole world changed. I didn't know much about what it meant until the funeral. I saw her in her casket. She was still and cold and stiff. They had patched her up, but I could see faint scars beneath the makeup on her face. There was a bullet wound somewhere in her chest that I couldn't see. I watched them lower her into the ground and I began to understand that I would never see her again in this life.*

xsweetxdreamsx: *The final letter came late in the post several weeks after the funeral. I guess it got lost somewhere along the way for a while. It was like a message from beyond the grave. It came with a poem that she'd intended for me to read before I went to sleep. She called it Sweet Dreams.*

My heart stops for a moment when I read the final message. I know I should have seen it coming, but it hurts all the same. Because she's just like me. She's had someone stolen from her too soon. Someone good, and pure, who deserved to live a long and happy life. Someone who spent their whole life protecting someone, or something, no matter what. This girl's story feels like staring in the mirror and seeing someone identical to you – not in looks, but in experience.

Vianne_Writes: *I'm so sorry. I know that's not enough, but I am.*

xsweetxdreamsx: *I miss her every day. It's like she's back on tour, but this time, I know she won't ever come back. But her letters keep her alive. It helps.*

I wish that Rita had left something like that behind. But then it occurs to me that I have something of hers. I fish in the drawer beside my bed for my iPod. I cradle it in my hands for a moment. I haven't used it since arriving here. It reminds me of the day it happened, when Rita and I shared earphones and listened to her band on the bus. But as I slowly unwind the earphones from around the device, I wonder if maybe this is what I need. To hear her again.

When the messenger notification pings again, I remember that I left Dream hanging. I shuffle back to my laptop to read the message.

xsweetxdreamsx: *Did you leave? I'm sorry. I know no one wants to hear sad stories.*

Vianne_Writes: *No, it's okay. Sad stories are kind of the only ones I know. I understand the need to talk sometimes.*

xsweetxdreamsx: *Do you? Want to talk, I mean? I'm all ears. It really helped, talking just then. Just imagine shouting into the void. It makes it less scary.*

It might be kind of good. To tell someone what happened. Not just what happened to Rita, but everything before that. About my parents and the life I lived with them. It was something I never fully disclosed to anyone outside of my family. They know the weight I carry around with me, but no one else does.

And now, I want to get these feelings off my chest. They've been weighing me down so long that I'm used to having a stone in my stomach. I want to talk to someone who knows what it's like to lose someone you love, to go through hardships that you wouldn't wish on anyone else. I want to tell it to someone so far away that I'll never truly feel attached to them. We'll never meet in person, and if we never speak again after tonight, who will she even tell my secrets to? Someone on the other side of the world?

Suddenly, I'm spilling every secret I've ever had to a girl I barely know. I don't know what she looks like. I don't know her surname. I don't know if anything she's told me is true. She could be a man. She could be underage, or sixty years old. I'll never know for sure. But I tell her everything. Every painful detail right from the start. And when I click send, I feel a little lighter. My heart is racing and my eyes are clouded over and I feel about as far away from reality as I can get, but I've done it.

I sit back on my pillows, biting my nails. I wonder if I've told her too much. Well, of course I have. It's not every day you tell everything to a total stranger. But that's kind of what happens in therapy, I guess. Except that therapy is face to face, and that makes it so much harder. But on the other hand, therapists are paid to listen to your messed-up life stories. Dream isn't. But after a few minutes, she sends me exactly what I need to hear.

xsweetxdreamsx: *I'm still here, I promise. I'm just writing a long reply.*

I sigh, hugging my pillow and closing my eyes while I wait for her message. It takes her a long time, but I don't mind. At least I know she's put thought into her reply. At least I know she's still there, bothering to reply after receiving one of the strangest messages of her life. It still comes as a little bit of a surprise when she replies, though. Gripping my pillow in case everything goes downhill, I lean in to read her message.

xsweetxdreamsx: *First of all, thank you for sharing with me. I've honoured that you put your trust in me. I know how hard it can be, and I understand why you opted to speak to me. It's a way of distancing yourself from the problem, right? With someone who doesn't know you and can't hurt you. And that's really great that you were able to tell me. But I really think that now you've had the courage to talk to me, you should talk to the other people in your life about it. I just told my boyfriend everything I told you last night and I feel a tonne lighter.*

xsweetxdreamsx: *You have such a large, supportive circle of women in your life. I know it's scary telling them something you've kept hidden for so long, but it'll be worth it. Trust me. These people have raised you. Not just Marigold, and Rita. Wilda has taken on a role too. Your sisters as well. Vanessa, it seems, has become such an important member of your team. From what you've told me, I think you really like this girl. And I think telling her all of this would make your friendship even stronger. Nothing blossoms without trust. Tell her what happened to you. Find a place where you feel safe to talk it over. After everything that's happened, it might help her see where you're coming from. You said the people you know don't always get it. This will help her see things from your point of view. What do you think?*

I think she's right. In fact, I know that she is. Before I change my mind, I send a text to Vanessa. I have to do this before I chicken out.

-Can you come over tomorrow? There's something I need to do.

SAFE SPACE

I spend the whole day preparing for what I have to tell Vanessa. She's heading here straight after college. I'm already starting to wish I didn't decide to bring all of this dirty laundry out of the basket.

I thought at first about having a day of relaxing, but when I ran a bath with my favourite oils, the smells reminded me of Rita's bath bombs. I drained the bath and tried to read, but the words swam in front of my eyes, suddenly senseless. It's the same when I try to write. I think about messaging Dream, but I know she'll be busy – she only messages me in the evenings.

I try to look calm as I head for the downstairs bathroom. I don't need Marigold or Wilda noticing how much I'm freaking out right now. A cloud of black sweeps over my eyes briefly. I'm not getting enough oxygen. I open the bathroom window even though it's pouring down with rain. I run the cold tap and put my wrists underneath to shock my system. I splash the water on my face several times, wincing, but it helps a bit. When I look in the mirror, I almost recoil.

Marigold is always telling me I look unhealthy, but this is the first time I've believed her. My skin is waxy and pale. My hair, damp from splashing my face, hangs limp around my face in a lifeless brown curtain. The skin around my eyes is dry from crying and rubbing at them. I run a hand over my face. It's rough and flaky to touch.

I stare for a long time at my face. In another life, I could probably look nice. I would have clear skin and freckles that resurface after long days in the sun. I might wear a little mascara to frame the eyes that Rita always told me were my best feature. My hand comes to rest under my chin and I close my eyes.

It's not a perfect world.

There's a knock on the door.

"Lori, is everything alright?" Wilda asks. "Would you like a glass of water?"

I lean over the sink, trying to catch my breath. "Yes please. I'll be out in a moment."

When I emerge, Wilda is waiting for me with a glass of water. I take it gratefully. Wilda opens her arms for a hug, and I realise I could really do with one. I let her pull me, my chin resting on her shoulder. Her frame is different to Rita's, but her curly hair brushing my face reminds me of her so much. Wilda feels my shoulders tense and misunderstands.

"It's okay. I know talking to Vanessa is going to be daunting, but we're all here for you. We're on your team."

She has no idea that I was thinking of Rita, but it helps. She has this unconditional love for us that I never expected. Even if we're not related by blood, I know that she treats me like she would Honey. She'd give the same kind of love to Rowena, if Ro would let her close

154

enough. She's given me more than my own birth parents ever did in the few months I've been here. Which is exactly what I'm about to explain to Vanessa.

Honey and Vanessa arrive back from college and Wilda lets me go, tapping my chin with her finger and smiling. She goes to the door to greet them while I take a moment to compose myself, sipping my water. This is it. This could change everything.

I head to the living room. Everyone is arranged on the sofa, talking quietly. It's almost comical how the mood changes when I enter. They all look up at once, words catching on their lips and forcing them into quiet. My vision blurs again and I hold on to the door frame for support. There's a gnawing in my stomach. It suddenly occurs to me that maybe I'm not ready to talk to Vanessa. It's like having a live audience for a one woman show. Except no one is going to applaud at the end. If anything, there will be tears. Or worse, silence.

I can't speak. Vanessa stands up slowly, approaching me like I'm a flighty animal. I feel like running right now, but where would I go? This house is currently the only place that doesn't automatically send me tumbling into a panic attack. Except now my lungs are constricted, my pulse is raised, and my eyes are dark. One of Vanessa's hands holds my waist, the other cradles my numb fingers.

"Shall we go upstairs?"

I nod. We move slowly upstairs. I feel cold all of a sudden, trying not to shiver. Vanessa seems to read my mind and wraps a blanket around my shoulders the second we sit down on my bed. She's still holding my hand.

"I'm sorry…I'm just a little on edge right now."

"Of course you are," Vanessa soothes, rubbing my back. "This is a big deal, Lori. I know I've been asking you for a while to open up to me…and I appreciate that you're doing this. But you don't have to. It's not too late."

"I want to…I have so much crowding my head. So much I want to talk about…I feel like you'll understand me better once you know."

"Then let's just take it slow, yeah? What can I do? To make this more comfortable for you? Do you have a routine for making a safe space?"

I nod. When I'm feeling at my worst, I surround myself with things that make me feel better. Blankets. A hot water bottle. A nice drink. Rita used to be a part of it too. She'd sit next to me quietly and wait for the panic to be over. But now it's just me here. I have to figure this out for myself.

I stand shakily to pull the curtains across, blocking out the light from outside. I keep the blanket wrapped around my shoulders as I prepare my electrical diffuser with a relaxing blend. I choose juniper and rosemary, a mix that Rita taught me to make for rejuvenation. It's a nod to her, and it makes me feel like she's still here with me. I close my eyes and breathe in. The blend makes my chest feel clear and light, even though my lungs are battling for breath.

"Better?" Vanessa asks me. I nod.

"A little. I…I just don't know where to start."

"Are you…are you going to tell me about your birth parents?"

I nod. Revisiting this part of my past is never easy.

"Before I joined this family…before I changed my name, I was Caitlin. My mum was Irish. She met my dad on St Patrick's Day at a party. She didn't mean to get pregnant with me, and they never got married."

I can't face looking at Vanessa so I stare down at my lap.

"They were violent people. They never actually hurt me, not deliberately, but they hit each other sometimes. Mostly they hit other people. They liked to get into fights, even with their so-called friends sometimes. They'd invite their friends over all the time. Most nights, really. I can remember barely ever sleeping at night. I'd hide away in the cupboard in my parent's room to get away from it all. Sometimes, people would come into the bedroom and take drugs. I don't know if they ever knew I was there. I'd stay quiet as much as I could and try to block it out. That was my reality for six years."

"Oh, Lori…"

I close my eyes for a moment, but I quickly open them again. I can picture the scene far too clearly when I close my eyes.

"One time, when I was six, they threw a party. They were out of it. They probably didn't know what they were doing. Well, some part of them did. But they weren't thinking straight. A fight happened and everyone was cheering it on, like it was some kind of game. I was locked away in the cupboard, shaking, just wishing it would be over. I wanted to call for help, but I didn't know how. One of the neighbours heard and called the police. But by the time they arrived…there was someone dying in our flat."

I'm shaking so hard now that I feel sick. It's a memory I've long ignored. But now that I've said it aloud, the reality of it comes raining down on my shoulders like rocks. I recall the officer who found me there that day. He had a kind face buried beneath a beard. He wiped tears from my face. He told me to bury my face in his chest so I couldn't see as he carried me out. But I looked. I had to know. And I saw my father…beaten and battered. I…I think he died of brain damage later that week. I was too numb at the time to remember what they told me. But I never saw my mother again. Sometimes I wonder if she was the one who did that to him. I don't think it was her. But even though I'd been locked away in the cupboard, trying to get away from it all…I wondered if it was my fault. My parents always made me feel as though I was a problem they hadn't figured out how to solve. They told me on more than one occasion that I ruined their lives. I wondered if their lives would've gone differently if they hadn't had me. Maybe they would've stopped partying. Maybe they would've waited longer to have kids, and had them with someone they truly cared about. Maybe I really did ruin their lives."

"Lori…don't say such a thing. After how they treated you…"

I shake my head. "I know it doesn't make sense. But nothing much has ever made sense in my life. And I've held on to those things they told me ever since because that's all I knew back then. I knew my life was falling apart and I knew that I was there through every second of it. So maybe I was to blame. Maybe I was the problem."

Vanessa reaches out for my hand. "No. You're not. I know you're not."

I swallow. It's all coming back to me. I take myself back to that dark room in my parent's flat. I feel the officer lift me up. My head turns. And I see my father lying there, his face on the ground. I guess it's a blessing that it's all a blur to me now. But it's stayed with me ever since. How could it not?

"I've spent so long trying to find little tricks to life that make it easier to bear," I whisper. "I've always been superstitious. I spent a long time convincing myself that there is magic in rituals and routine. Never stepping on cracks in the pavement, never walking under a ladder. I freaked out once when I dropped a mirror and watched it crack. I stayed home every Friday the 13th, just in case. I guess it all fed into my obsessions, my anxiety. I thought those things might keep me safe. And it kept me going for most of my life, even if failing those rituals scared me out of my wits. I started to believe that it was working, that I had power over what happened to me. I wished…I wished for a family, and I found one. It was all coming together. But then Rita was taken from me…and I realised I'd been living in a lie. There's no third time lucky. You think birthday candle wishes will last, that crossing your fingers and your toes and your arms will stop bad things from happening, but it's not like that. Bad things happen. And wishing for things to stay the same didn't stop Rita being killed. The little control I thought I had over my life…it left me when she did."

Vanessa hugs me now and I bury my face in her neck. I don't want to cry, but it feels impossible not to. I grip her and it only makes her hold me harder.

"It makes sense," she whispers to me. "I don't think anyone could ever blame you for feeling this way. You're braver than you give yourself credit for, Lori. I don't know how I would have coped with everything you've been through. I'm proud of you."

I let out a breath. It feels like I've been holding it for years. But it feels relieving to talk about it now, to get it off my chest. I never thought anybody outside of my family would want to hear what I have to say. Vanessa didn't have to stay. She could've run at any time and never looked back. But she stays with me. She stays and she holds me because she knows how much I need it right now.

She knows how much I need *her*.

ATTIC

The nightmares began the night after I told Vanessa everything. I went to sleep feeling lighter, but woke with worry weighing my chest down, images from the dream still clinging to the air in front of my eyes. It's a recurring nightmare I remember having as a child – except it's real. It's like I'm running through all of my bad memories, escaping one and being hit by another. I run through my parent's flat, through all the kid's homes I endured, looking for a way out. But now the dream has a different ending. I'm out of breath from running, but I've nearly reached our old home. Rita and Marigold stand on the front door step, waving. I reach out to them, almost there. And then I fall through the ground, faster and faster, until I plonk back on my bed in my birth parent's apartment.

So I stop sleeping. I feel more awake in the night time than I do when daylight streams through the window. I often cross paths with Rowena in the night when I go to grab a glass of water. Every evening, she tells me I should drink coffee, and every night I decline the offer – no matter how tired I am, I still can't stand the taste.

The days aren't all bad. In fact, things are better now than they've been in weeks. Vanessa always messages me in the mornings on the bus, and then again when she's on her way home. The messages from Dream come later on, usually after dinner when Honey settles down to do her homework. We sit together now, me in my alcove, Honey at the desk, typing away on our laptops and occasionally having snippets of conversation. It makes me feel sociable. I've never been much of a talker but now, when Vanessa and Dream message me, I'm eager to reply within seconds. On the nights when Rowena actually gets some shut eye, I always have Dream to keep me occupied. Things could be better. But things are okay.

Christmas comes and goes. None of us felt like making a fuss this year, so I just cooked dinner and we ate around the table and exchanged a few small gifts. On New Year's Eve, everyone goes to bed before midnight, but no one sleeps. Now it's January, and it's back to our version of ordinary, which isn't ordinary at all.

But the slithers of light through the darkness keep us all going. For me, mostly it's Vanessa. She has taken my worries and anxiety in her stride, too. Every few days, she comes over with a gift, or texts me an idea for controlling anxiety attacks. She bought me a bottle of bubbles last week after reading somewhere that they can be good during a panic attack, that blowing them controls your breathing. But today, she texted me to say she has another surprise. It's Saturday morning, and she's made me close my eyes and wait upstairs while she brings the gift to me. I hear it rattling as she climbs the stairs.

"Let me see!" Rowena says, stomping out of her bedroom while I remain in mine, my hands covering my eyes. I hear her gasp. "That's so cool!"

I know now that it must be a good present; Ro doesn't get easily excited. Vanessa places the present on my lap. It's heavy and digs into my legs. I furrow my brow, trying to figure out what it could be.

"Stop guessing and open your eyes!" Vanessa says. The first thing I see is Rowena hovering by the door, grinning. Then I see why; on my lap rests a cage. Inside, a tiny brown hamster sits, staring up at me inquisitively. I gasp, overwhelmed by a sudden need to scoop it in my hands and nuzzle it.

"Can I hold it, Lori?" Rowena pleads. I smile, opening the cage and nodding to Rowena. I don't think I've ever seen her so happy. She approaches with wide eyes, her usual angry façade replaced with soft features as she gently picks the hamster up. She brings it to her eye level and gasps in delight, her hands cupping around it in a protective bubble. She looks up at Vanessa.

"Is it a boy or a girl?"

"A boy. I thought a boy would be nice in a house of girls." She turns to me. "I've heard that having a pet can help with anxiety attacks. I read a bunch of articles about it."

"This is so lovely. And so thoughtful," I whisper, blushing. Vanessa grins, sitting next to me on the bed. Our legs are almost touching and my face grows redder.

"What's he called?" Rowena asks.

"Well, that's up to Lori!" Vanessa says, catching my eye. I see Rowena droop a little, and I feel bad. I can't bear to see her look so sad after her burst of happiness.

"Why don't we all come up with a few ideas?" I suggest. Rowena nods furiously.

"Okay. I'm going to come up with a really good one."

"How about Pantoufle?" Vanessa says. Rowena wrinkles her nose.

"Is that a real word?"

"It's French," Honey pipes up from her perch at the desk. I'd forgotten she was even in the room. She's not even looking at us, hunched over her books. She sits there so often that she's begun to complain of neck ache. "It means slipper."

I know why Vanessa picked it, and I give her a sideways smile to let her know I appreciate her reference. Pantoufle is an imaginary rabbit in the Chocolat novel. But Rowena doesn't seem so keen.

"This hamster isn't French. He's English to the core. I bet he lifts his pinky finger to drink tea."

Vanessa snorts, and Rowena strokes the hamster thoughtfully. "I think he deserves something regal, like Henry or Phillip."

"Really, Ro? You'll make him sound like a middle-aged man, not a hamster," Honey says, rolling her eyes.

There's a lot of arguing before somewhere along the way, someone suggests sarcastically that we call him Hammy, and the name sticks. But not just Hammy; at Rowena's request, he's now King Hammy the third of Lancashire. Where the first and second Hammy came from, I have no idea.

Vanessa stays for a few hours, chatting to me while Rowena and I take it in turns petting Hammy. He gets bored of our endless snuggles eventually and nips my hand to let me know he's ready to go back in his cage.

Honey stares at the cage for a while and I can tell she's not pleased about something.

"What's wrong, Honey?"

She purses her lips. "I don't want to be a killjoy. But do we have to keep it in here?"

"He's not an it!" Rowena snaps.

"Fine. He. Do we have to keep *him* in here?"

"Where else would he go?"

"I don't know, Lori. Somewhere where humans don't have to sleep. He's noisy, and he smells. Maybe Wilda will let us have him in the living room."

"No need. He can go in my bedroom," Rowena insists. "You can come and visit him all the time, Lori. You can play with him all day when I'm out, and then we can have Hammy Hour! Get it? Like Happy Hour?"

"Ro, Happy Hour is an excuse for people to get drunk on cheap cocktails, not play with hamsters," Honey says, but she smiles wearily. Rowena looks up at me with wide eyes.

"Please, Lori?"

She's smiling so much that even if Honey hadn't demanded Hammy's removal, I probably would have let her keep him there. I smile, leaning to pet the top of Hammy's tiny head through the top of the cage.

"Of course. As long as I have visitation rights. And you can scoop his poop."

She rolls her eyes, but she's smiling. She gently picks up Hammy's cage and moves him through to her bedroom. For once, she doesn't slam the door behind her. She leaves it open, and I watch as she places Hammy's cage on top of her dresser. Vanessa smiles at her fondly.

"You have the cutest family," Vanessa says. I smile. "I do."

Honey doesn't look up from her homework, but I catch her smiling. Vanessa stands up, brushing a stray bit of straw from Hammy's cage onto the floor. Then, with a guilty glance at Honey, she picks it up and puts it in the bin.

"I should go and do some homework. See me out?"

Vanessa practically skips down the stairs. Wilda and Marigold are in the kitchen, and they look up as we pass. They look smug, like they know something they shouldn't.

"I take it the hamster went down well?" Wilda says, smiling.

"It sure did, Wilda. If you want to play with him, you might have to prise him away from Ro. She got attached very quickly."

"If it's in Rowena's room, I'll never see it again," Wilda says with a tired smile. Vanessa catches my eye.

"Not if she hears you calling him 'it'," Vanessa replies. She grabs me and pulls me in, rocking us back and forth in the most energetic hug I've ever had.

"See you tomorrow, Lori. Look after King Hammy."

I watch her leave with a smile, waiting until she's crossed the road safely before closing the door. Marigold and Wilda give me knowing smiles as I walk past them.

"Did you have a nice time with Vanessa?" Marigold asks smugly. I roll my eyes, but I can't help but smile. If even they can see sparks between Vanessa and I, maybe it's possible I have a chance with her.

Dinner starts with a good feeling between us all. Everyone is at the table, and everyone is chatting. Rowena even manages to say a few kind words to Wilda, which puts a smile on both of their faces. Wilda finishes before the rest of us and turns her attention to me.

"Lori, do you have a couple of hours spare? I was thinking tomorrow when I'm off work you could help me with clearing out the attic. I think now that there's a full house, I should think about making some more space. I've got plans to clear out the garage and basement too, and then I thought we could do a garden sale. What do you think?"

I think she's probably easing me into the idea of going outside for the garage sale, which is the last thing I want to do. I've barely even set foot at the back of the house since we moved here. The last time was to eat dinner on the patio, but that was months ago now. I don't mention this, though. I can let her think she's won for a while. It might put Marigold at ease too. It's a great opportunity for Mari as well – getting rid of her possessions is on her bucket list. She seems to be thinking the same thing when she catches my eye.

"I think it's a great idea," she says. "I'm sure Lori would be more than happy to help, now that she's improving."

Improving? Does she really think that since I told them about my past that I'm *improving?* I guess she has no clue I haven't been sleeping. Not that I'm about to tell her if she hasn't noticed. She holds my gaze for a little longer and I frown. I watch as she sets down her cutlery, and I get the sense that the mood is shifting. "Actually, that leads me to something I've wanted to mention for a little while."

I'm suddenly nervous. I know what she's about to say. She's going to tell them about the list. It's been several months now since she first told me about it. She hasn't even mentioned it since, though there's been something hanging in the air between us. I was starting to think maybe she'd decided it was a bad idea. But now I see that she was just waiting for the right time. Now that Christmas has been and gone, maybe she thinks it's a good time to make her move. She glances around at everyone, her hands pressed together.

"I've decided…I'll be going away for a while. To Croatia. I've spoken to your Aunt Wilda, and she's said she can look after you while I'm gone. It won't be for long, but this is something I have to do."

The whole room is silent for a moment. Even Rowena, who isn't easily fazed, looks shocked.

"Like on a holiday?" she says in disbelief.

"No! Not a holiday."

"Good. Because you know how ludicrous that would be, right? Leaving us to go on a holiday? This better be good."

Marigold looks nervous, and rightly so. Rowena is glaring at her, crunching loudly on her salad. It gives her the appearance of an angry rabbit.

"It is. Good, I mean." Marigold takes a deep breath. She seems to put her whole body into it, her back rising as her chest does. "Rita left me a letter. She has a list of things that she wants me to do. She wants me to go and volunteer abroad and do a charity skydive, among other things. I've budgeted it all and the best option seems to be Croatia. I've completed the majority of the other things on the list, and I feel that the only way for me to move on is for me to finish the rest. That's why I have to go."

Rowena stares at her. "Oh. Right. Of course. Makes sense. We're holding you back from moving on. So you have to go on a little holiday to sort yourself out. Right?"

"No, Rowena…"

"Don't be so cruel," Honey says, her lip trembling. "Mum is clearly just saying that she has to do what Rita would have wanted."

"So Rita wanted her to abandon us, just when we might be starting to heal? Rita would never have said that. She would have told Marigold to stick around for the sake of her kids, no matter how much she was hurting." For the first time since everything fell apart, I see tears in Ro's eyes. She didn't even cry at the funeral, her face stoic and cold throughout, but now tears well in her eyes, and I remember that she's only human. For all I know, she cries herself to sleep every night. I watch her hands curl into fists and I'm scared she might punch something. She's done worse before. But she doesn't. As she releases the tension in her hands, her tears begin to fall and she crumbles. We all watch in amazement as she rises from her seat, keeping cold eye contact with Marigold. "We lost one Mum. We don't need to lose you too. Hell, me and Lori have lost everyone, but you. I thought you'd get that." She snorts through her tears. "You're all the same. Selfish as hell. You know what? You go on your little trip. Just don't expect me to welcome you back."

With that, Rowena leaves the room. I want to go after her, but I know she'd only shut me out. The hurt in her eyes is something I won't forget in a hurry. Honey reaches for Marigold's hand, both of them tearing up.

"I understand," she says, with a nod as though to affirm her point. "You should go. See this through. We'll be okay."

Speak for yourself, I want to tell her. But this family is fragile enough as it is. One little push, and we'll all be tumbling over the edge. So I keep quiet and tell myself to stop being selfish. For once, Marigold is making this about her, and I know that if I were in her shoes, I'd do the same without blinking an eye.

But it won't make her leaving any easier.

It takes Wilda all of Saturday morning to find her ladder in the garage so that we can get up into the attic. Then she has to clear some boxes out of the way so that we can actually get up there. She descends the ladder, sneezing three times in a row.

"It's pretty dusty up there. It definitely needs a good clean before we put anything back up there."

Honey peers up the ladder, her nose wrinkled as grey clusters float from inside. "When did you last go up there? It shouldn't be this bad."

"It's been years, Honey. I've just never found time, I guess. It's mostly junk up there. I guess I've just shoved stuff up there to keep the rest of the house tidy. I'm sure most of it can be thrown away or sold. It's not like I've missed it." She claps her hands together. "Right, Lori. Time to enter the cave. Do you want to help, Honey?"

She shakes her head, raising her mug of coffee. She's holding a packet of pills in her other hand. She keeps complaining of headaches lately. "Nope. Study time."

"Of course. If you do have a spare minute, feel free to join us!"

I get the feeling that the last thing Honey wants to do with her free time is look through some old boxes with enough dust on them to make a whole village sneeze. Even I'm beginning to regret helping. But attics are notorious for holding one thing – family history. I'd be lying if I said I wasn't curious about Wilda's past.

Plus, Wilda's past is full of Rita. I wouldn't pass up an opportunity to find a connection to her.

My legs shake as I climb the ladder, even though Wilda's holding it steady at the bottom. I'm glad when I reach the top even though it's dark and smells strange. Wilda follows me up, clicking a torch on and off several times.

"Perfect. You can use this. So if you find any clothes, or ornaments…anything non sentimental, send it down to me. We can hopefully get this mess sorted in an afternoon, and do the sale next weekend. I'm going to start sorting through some of the boxes downstairs. There's no sense in us both stumbling around up here. No need to spend hours up here, either. Just be in and out, yeah?"

I wish she'd let me sort the boxes downstairs. It's horrible up here. But I promised to help, so I may as well get stuck in. Besides, this is the least I can do for her when she's given me a house and a home.

"I'll get right on it."

I make a half-hearted attempt at sorting through a few boxes, knowing that soon enough, Vanessa will come and save me from the boredom. Her weekends are mostly spent here now, and it keeps me sane. It'll be good to have her here today after the big fight between Marigold and Rowena last night.

I hear Vanessa arrive at around one o'clock. She sounds her usual cheery self as she chats with Wilda for a bit. Before long, I hear her boots thudding up the stairs.

"Lori, you didn't tell me we were attic hunting!" she shouts up the ladder. "I'm so stoked for this. It's my dream come true. Help me up, will you?"

Vanessa practically hops up each step of the ladder, and I reach out to grab her hand, scared of her falling. She laughs at my expression.

"I wasn't going to fall. Even if I did, I wouldn't fall far." She pokes my ribs. "You don't have to worry about me. I'm practically a cat. Nine lives, baby. And springy feet."

"You didn't sound so springy when you came stomping up the stairs just then."

"Ouch. Someone's grouchy. What's wrong, missy? Bad morning?"

I sigh, shaking my head at myself. Why am I being so rude?

"Not so much this morning…but last night was…well, it was a bit of a nightmare, to be honest. Sorry for snapping."

"Hey, you know I take it like a champ. Go on. You can tell me about it while we look through some of this stuff. But trust me. This will cheer you up. I bet Wilda has a treasure trove up here. We're like attic pirates."

I know she's trying to cheer me up, but I'm not in the mood for her chirpy kookiness. For once, I need her to take things a bit more seriously.

"Marigold is finally going away."

"Oh, Lori, that's awful. I'm sorry, I wouldn't have made those stupid jokes if I had known."

"It's okay, I'm alright. I mean, I'm not really…I know she needs to do this for herself, and for Rita, but I need her here. Not that she's been so great recently. I think maybe it'll be better, once she comes back. She'll have some time to get herself together. Then she'll be able to support me better. Honey and Ro, too."

"But it won't necessarily work like that, will it? I mean, it's like people going travelling to 'find themselves.' What if they don't find what they're looking for? What if all they find out is that they've wasted a bunch of money on a really expensive holiday?"

I wish she wouldn't say things like that. It's not helping at all. It's making things worse. "Yeah, but Marigold is doing this with good reason. She's got a purpose. The list…"

"I know. But she might come home and discover that she's finished the list, but she doesn't feel any better. She's not just going to get over something like this in a day."

"But it's got to be worth a shot. At least she has something to keep her busy."

Vanessa is quiet, and I know she's wondering if she's about to overstep a line. I straighten up, almost banging my head.

"What is it? What are you thinking about?"

Vanessa chews her lip. "I just wondered if, you know…you'd ever thought about ways that you might move on too."

"What do you mean?"

"Well, I know you said Marigold hasn't found a suitable therapist yet, but…but there are options, you know? I've looked into it. I thought maybe you could try one of those websites. You can talk to someone at any time, it's all anonymous. It's really good for people who are just being introduced to the idea of therapy-"

"I appreciate the thought, Vanessa, but I don't want you looking at therapists for me."

"But I worry about you, babe. It's all about looking to the future. What do you want for the future?"

I can't tell her that some days, I can't even think of a week ahead, let alone years. There's days where I spend hours on the edge of a panic attack for no reason at all, shaking quietly in my room so I don't disrupt the household from their day to day activities. The activities my body sometimes just can't handle, shuddering at the thought of doing things most people do without a second thought. It's not something I can tell her, though. She'd only tell me that's exactly the reason I need help.

"I'm just…I'm taking time. To figure out what I'm supposed to do with myself. I don't need anything else. Just some space and time."

Vanessa nods, but she won't look at me. I decide to swerve the topic completely. She can't keep this talk up all day. I make myself busy rooting through a box of men's clothes. I can't figure out why Wilda has men's clothes in her attic, but I guess it's not my place to ask.

"This can all go on the sell pile. It's no use to anyone."

"Lori…"

"I know you're trying to help, but I'd really like it if we could drop this for today. I've got enough on my plate."

"Okay. Fair enough. But I want to talk to you about this. It's important."

I don't think she means to be, but she sounds patronising. I just nod to keep her appeased, knowing this is a topic I'd be happy to avoid forever. Of course, someone like her will never understand why I can't do the things she does. She's happy and healthy. She's confident, well-liked, bubbly, sweet. One glance at her big blue eyes and I'm good for nothing. But I'm not like her, and I can handle that. I'm just not sure she can.

Vanessa lets it go and I know I can't dwell on the conversation if I'm going to have a good day. I pack it away in the corner of my mind and carry on rooting through the boxes.

"Lori, get over here. This box is so cute."

I turn around and see Vanessa holding up Wilda's wedding dress. I recognise it from the wedding photos in the dining room. It's a little crumpled, but the colours haven't faded out. I can see now that it's made of tulle, giving it the floaty feel of a fairy princess gown. I shuffle to hold it in my hands. It's a work of art.

"I just know she was a beautiful bride. Shall we hunt for photos?"

I'm not sure how I feel about digging into Wilda's wedding box. I don't know much about why she split from her husband – only that he's long gone with a new family now. It occurs to me that maybe the clothes I found are his, and Wilda has kept them all this time. It's a sad thought, but I can't deny I would like to see more of her wedding, especially since Rita was the maid of honour.

Vanessa pulls out a handmade album, its pages bulging with photos. I can't resist. We sit cross-legged with the book resting on both our knees. Vanessa turns each page with care. She flicks quicker than I'd like, and I find myself touching her hand to slow her down, trying to ignore the electricity on my fingertips. The first few pages are just of Wilda and her husband, but Rita and Marigold are on these pages. Marigold hasn't changed a bit. Her hand is locked on Rita's arm, her posture stiff and a little nervous. She's not a bridesmaid, but she fits in perfectly with the pastel theme, wearing a dress that matches her watery eyes. Rita looks a little wrong in her purple dress. It's a change from her usual attire. She often stuck to simple clothes – black, white and denim. It suited her. This dress is the wrong colour, the wrong style, the wrong length for her short legs. But she's smiling, and I know she's wearing it because that was what Wilda wanted. A perfect dress for her perfect pastel wedding.

I spend a happy half hour looking through the wedding box. There are all sorts of things in here – a blue braid anklet that was definitely made by Marigold. A cake topper depicting a married man and woman. A whole bunch of 'just married' junk. I can't imagine Wilda wanting to keep this stuff, though. Her house is so free of sentimental clutter, and now I know why – it's all catching dust up here.

"She never talks about him," I say as we pause on a photo of Wilda and her husband, whose name I don't even know.

"Would you, if the love of your life left you?"

I close the book. I'm starting to see why Wilda didn't want us lingering up here. "I think we should put it back."

"Me too."

There's another box that catches my eye. It's placed right in the corner, as though to keep it as far out of the way as possible. Vanessa catches me looking and raises an eyebrow.

"Out of sight, out of mind?"

I know that if that is the reason Wilda put it away in the corner, then I shouldn't be looking in it. But she gave me free reign of the attic. She told me to sort through the boxes. I pick it up and give it a light shake. It's light as a feather. I look at Vanessa and she nods, as curious as I am to see what's inside.

Inside the box are several thin plastic folders. They each contain some kind of document. I feel my stomach twist. Something feels wrong about opening the folders. But I can't help myself. I slide out the document.

"What is it, Lori?"

I feel sick to my stomach. "It's…a birth certificate."

I already know what the document beneath it is, but I still look at it. I have to confirm my suspicions. I sink down to the floor.

"And…a death certificate."

There are three folders, but I don't dare look at the others. The first one was bad enough. I look at the dates on the certificates, trying not to notice the names at the top of each. Knowing the names would make it so much worse.

"…her baby died two days after it was born."

Vanessa gasps, turning away from me. But I can't look away the way she can. This is my family history. I cradle the certificate in my hand. I imagine Wilda holding her baby in a single palm, it's skin red raw and scrunched as it cries. I imagine her praying that her child will make it past the first twenty-four hours. Three times over. That's surely what the other folders hold. I don't need to look to know. *Bad things come in threes, the* voice in the back of my head whispers. These lightweight folders are heavy with loss. I clutch it to my chest. The brief histories of my would-be cousins are in my hands. And suddenly, I understand Wilda a whole lot better. I know now why she's so desperate to cling to our family. Her children are gone. Her husband has gone, presumably because he couldn't handle what they went through. Now her sister's gone too. We're all she has. I knew that before, but now it really hits home. I think of how lonely she must have been. I wonder if Rita knew all of this. Did she know that every time Wilda came over, she was wishing for what Rita had? Suddenly I can see how much of a blessing we were upon her. Even though she lost a sister, she gained a family. And in that respect, Wilda and I are exactly alike.

By the time I notice the footsteps on the ladder, it's too late to hide the folders.

"Girls! I just wanted to check if-"

Wilda stops at the top of the ladder. Her torch finds me in the dark corner like a spotlight. She spots me cradling the folders and her face falls. I try to swallow, but there's a lump in my throat.

"Wilda, I-"

"You weren't to know," Wilda says quickly. She doesn't meet my eye. "If you wouldn't mind putting the folders back…"

I nod, feeling terrible. I turn my back to put the folder back in the box, and when I turn around, Wilda is already disappearing down the ladder.

BASEMENT

It's a few days since Wilda caught me in the attic, and it's been pretty quiet in the house. I don't think Wilda is angry at me, but she's withdrawn. She's at work most of the day anyway, but even at dinner, she barely says two words to me. No one says much, really. Honey is barely present, study guides rested on her lap so she's staring down while she eats. Rowena has started eating dinner in her room, and it doesn't surprise me much. She's not exactly the biggest fan of either Marigold or Wilda right now.

And now, Marigold is standing by the door with her luggage, ready to leave for her trip, and Rowena is nowhere to be seen.

The rest of us are gathered around the front door. Marigold's hands are clutching the pulley on her suitcase. She keeps her gaze low so I can't tell if there are tears in her eyes. We've called up to Rowena several times with no response. Marigold shifts her feet.

"Well, I can't wait forever," she says with a quiet sniff. "If she doesn't want to say goodbye, I can't force her."

"Let me try her room one more time," I say. Marigold nods gratefully to me as I leave the room, heading upstairs. There's no light coming from underneath the door. I bet she hasn't even opened her curtains. I rap on the door.

"Rowena. You should come and say goodbye. Marigold is leaving."

"I'm not coming."

I'm surprised she even replied. I sigh, leaning against the door frame. "Rowena, I know you're upset, but you don't want her to go on a sour note, do you?"

"I do, actually. And tell her to hurry up. I'm not leaving my room until she's gone, and I really need a wee."

"You're being childish."

"Don't talk to me about childishness."

I blink. "What do you mean?"

"Go figure. And leave me alone."

I know that once Ro has made up her mind, there's not much that will change it. I hear her muttering to Hammy and decide it's better to abandon ship. I'm still confused about her comment, but I brush it off. Now is the time to focus on goodbyes.

Marigold and Honey are hugging when I get to the porch. I stand beside Wilda, giving them some space to get through their goodbyes.

"Be good, Honey. Don't work too hard. I know how you stress."

"*Mum.*"

"If it becomes too much, just talk to the college. They'll help you out. You can always drop a subject, or even two."

Honey pulls out of Marigold's grasp, rubbing her arm. "I said I'll be okay."

"I know, I just worry," Marigold says. I shift from foot to foot. If she's worried about Honey, what does she feel about me? She turns to me and looks a little pained. I put on a brave face, but I'm praying that she might change her mind at the last minute. When she pulls me in and holds me hard, I know she's not going to.

"When I get home, I'm going to throw everything into getting you better. I swear it." She kisses the top of my head and I think she's done, but she still holds on to me.

"You'll call me if you need anything, won't you? Any little worry, or question, or thought. You'll call me, won't you?"

I nod to appease her, but I won't. She's got enough on her mind. This is her time, the time she's taking to recover. When she comes back, she can be a parent again. That's what I hope anyway. She squeezes me harder. I can barely breathe, but I'd rather hold this position than watch her go. Inevitably, though, she lets go. She opens the porch door, and I feel the cold air hit me hard. It's been a while since I felt the outside air. Wilda closes the door behind Marigold and the three of us crowd in the porch to watch her get in her taxi. I'm scared that Wilda's cool attitude will continue, but she puts a comforting arm around me and I relax a little. Things aren't right. Far from it. But knowing I still have Wilda makes me realise I'm safe, at least.

That's got to count for something.

Most people don't like basements. I guess they've got a bad reputation – they never play a good role in horror movies, after all. But I've spent all morning down here, and it's actually quite peaceful. Wilda hasn't given me any specific instructions for sorting through these boxes, so I can only assume I won't stumble across any more sensitive items. I hope, at least.

It hits four thirty and I get a text from Vanessa. She must nearly be home from college. The thought cheers me up slightly.

-Hey, Lori. Need some help in the basement?

-Sure. Come on over. Bring some gloves. There's a wicked stain I need to scrub, and we don't have any gloves.

-Wow. You know how to excite a girl.

Vanessa arrives several minutes later, armed with fresh chocolate cookies and a pair of yellow marigold gloves. She gives me a long hug and breaks off a bit of cookie, poking it through my lips and into my mouth.

"Chew," she instructs. I do as she asks. I know the philosophy behind her thinking – chocolate solves everything. She nibbles a cookie herself.

"How are you holding up?"

"I'm fine. I just feel a little numb. It's not hit me that she's gone yet. I don't even want to think about it, really."

"Consider your mind taken off it. Your fairy godmother is here to make all your wishes come true." She pauses, her face falling. "And listen…I'm so sorry about the other day. You know. In the attic. I thought it was best to get out of there so you and Wilda could talk."

"It's okay. I understand."

"Have you spoken to her yet?"

"No. There…the time hasn't seemed right."

Vanessa nods. "I know what you mean. It's such a big topic to bring up. But you guys will be okay. Wilda probably just needs some time to mull it over. She's been hiding this secret for years. She probably didn't expect you to stumble across it."

"For sure. I'll know when she's ready to talk. We can broach the topic then."

Vanessa nods with a smile. "I know you can get through it. Your family is tough as nails."

I smile, watching her stuff the rest of the cookie in her mouth and preparing for a battle with the sink in the corner by sliding the gloves on.

"I can do that."

"No need. I find it very satisfying cleaning something really dirty."

"Strange."

"Don't lie. You feel it too. You're jealous that I stole your job."

I smile at her ridiculousness. It never fails to make me smile. I move the final boxes upstairs and then sweep the floor. By the time I've swept up the excess, the basement is practically empty. The only things Wilda wanted to keep remain in a pile in the corner, plus a set of drums and an old guitar of Rita's. Vanessa peels off her gloves, putting her hands on her hips in satisfaction.

"Hey. Not bad for a day's work."

"Not bad at all."

Vanessa heads to the pile of stuff in the corner, her hand running over the drum set.

"I can't imagine Wilda jamming."

I smile, joining her behind the drum set. "Rita told me she and Wilda used to be in a band as kids. Or that's what they called it. I think it was when they were very little, before Rita even learned to play the guitar properly."

Vanessa picks up the guitar. She looks to me for permission. "Do you mind?"

"Go for it."

Vanessa grins. "You've never heard me play guitar."

"I haven't."

"I'm notoriously bad at it."

"So your Mum tells me."

"Hey! Mums are meant to say that their children are good at everything. Even if they're actually terrible."

"I guess it doesn't count if you're aware that you're bad."

Vanessa laughs, sitting on the drum stool and resting the guitar on her knee. "At least I can carry a tune, for the most part."

Vanessa starts to strum the guitar clumsily, something vaguely resembling a tune filling the air. She hums and it's tuneful – just not in tune with the guitar. She winces at the sound.

"I think the guitar needs tuning. I have no clue how you do that though."

"No wonder it sounds bad when you play it," I say, prising it from her fingers. I pull up a chair and sit down to retune the guitar. I fiddle with the tuning pegs for a while, plucking the strings occasionally to check the sound.

"You play? You never told me that."

I shake my head. "I used to, a little. Rita was always trying to get us into music. Rowena was terrible. She demanded trumpet lessons for a while and none of us slept for months."

Vanessa laughs. "Why doesn't that surprise me in the slightest?"

"Honey played classical piano for years. She was good, too. But when she hit college, she stopped. She said her studies were more important. It nearly broke Rita's heart."

"So what about you?"

I shrug. "I learned quickly. Rita was a good teacher. But I just preferred to listen to her. She'd show me a tune on the guitar and I'd rather have watched her do it than me. She made an art of it. There was just something right about it."

"Like when someone is a natural born writer."

"Yeah. Just like that."

I start playing a song I know she'll like. It's a soft acoustic version of a Gabrielle Aplin song. One of the last ones that Rita taught me. Vanessa recognises it right away. I knew she would – it's one of the songs I heard her humming on the bus. She starts to mouth the words as I play. She giggles when she realises I'm watching her. She starts to sing properly near the chorus. I revel in her voice, barely concentrating on the guitar. She closes her eyes and smiles when she sings. When she hits a high note, her eyebrows raise, and her hands seem to move with her crescendo. It's so soulful that I stop playing just to listen to her. It's like the days where I'd watch Rita at her concerts. I never thought I'd feel this way about music again. But I do right now.

She stops at the end of the chorus. She looks a little flushed, almost as though she's embarrassed.

"Whoops. Heh. Got a bit carried away there." She lowers her gaze, smiling shyly. "I'll bet you've not heard me sing either."

I rest the guitar against the wall gently. "I have. Heard you sing, I mean."

Vanessa cocks her head. "Really? I don't remember ever having sung in front of you. I think I would have remembered." Before I can reply, she continues on one of her tangents. "I sing all the time at home. Can't stop me. I do it without noticing. It drives everyone up the wall. Mum even caught me singing in my sleep once, but I don't think that's possible in this case…"

I smile. She seems nervous. As though something about this day has thrown her. I decide to throw her a bone.

"The day I first saw you. That day I fainted in class. You were singing on the bus. Well, humming really. Right behind me."

"I was?"

"Yeah. I remember the songs you listened to. I remember it all. I was so nervous that day, but something about hearing you humming on the bus…it calmed me down. I'm not sure I would have gotten through that bus journey without listening to you."

Vanessa looks surprised. It's a look I've never seen her wear before. It's cute. Really cute.

"That's so nice, Lori. I wish I'd have known that. I wish I'd known you back then. Maybe I could've stuck by you. Helped you through that day. Then maybe…maybe you would've been okay."

I sigh. "Vanessa, no. This was going to happen, sooner or later. I'm a mess. I've always been a mess."

Her hand moves to my cheek and I almost jump away. The gesture is so surprising that I even know how to process it.

"You're not a mess," she says quietly. Her thumb traces my cheekbone and I resist the urge to shiver. I don't want her to move away. "Don't ever tell yourself you're a mess. You're not."

She stands up for a moment, her hand leaving my skin for a brief moment. Then she perches herself on my knee, resting her forehead against mine.

"Is this okay?" she asks. I can't speak, but I manage to nod. I move my hands slowly to her waist. I'm scared that if I move too fast, this whole scene will fall apart and I'll realise it's just a pipedream. But when Vanessa's finger rests under my chin and tilts my head upwards, my heart is beating so fast that I know this must be real. She gives me the softest smile, brushing a thumb over my lip.

"Close your eyes, Lori."

I let her lead the way. I've never been kissed before. Her lips are soft, tender, tentative for a moment. But when she realises I'm not going to move away, her kiss becomes more wild, more uninhibited. Her hand grips the back of my head as though to hold me there, but I'm not going anywhere. There's so much I want to do. I want to feel her hair in my hands. I want to trail a hand down her back and feel her body react to my touch. But more than anything, I want to stay here, in this moment. I've waited for this. I've waited for her. And now that she's here, I can't bear the thought of letting go.

Vanessa's lips move from mine, only to shower kisses over my face. I laugh, wrapping my arms around her and pulling her closer to my chest. She strokes my hair as she smiles at me.

"I've been keeping that in for a while," Vanessa tells me. I crane my neck to kiss her again. The moment that it lasts is bliss.

"Me too."

"Can I kiss you again?"

I smile. "You don't ever have to ask."

GARDEN

The morning of the garden sale, I hear Wilda shuffling around at six am, beginning the preparations. I can feel sleep weighing down my eyes – I only drifted off a few hours ago. I try to go back to sleep, but twenty minutes passes and I realise it's not going to happen. Now that I know Wilda's awake, it's impossible to go back to sleep. I decide that while the rest of the house is still dormant, it might be a good time to speak to her. Now that Marigold's gone, it's more important than ever that we're on good terms.

To be honest, I miss Wilda. We've grown close since living here. She respects my needs and she listens to what I'm telling her. Sometimes I think she understands me better than Marigold. Somehow, we – two completely different people – click. Just like me and Rita did.

I pad downstairs, careful not to wake Honey or Rowena. Wilda has the side door in the kitchen wide open, the boxes for the sale stacked precariously. She attempts to lift a heavy box, grunting with the effort.

"Need any help?"

Wilda jumps at the sound of my voice, dropping the box on her foot. She winces.

"You scared the life out of me, Lori. Quiet as a mouse, you are."

"I'm so sorry…"

I pick the box up, staring at her foot and trying to figure out if I've done any lasting damage. I'll never forgive myself if I have. Wilda catches me watching and shakes her head with a brief chuckle.

"I'm fine, Lori. And yes. You can give me a hand. That would be great."

I hesitate a little on the step leading into the yard. I haven't been outside since we last had our dinner on the patio. It doesn't feel as scary as going to college, or walking near the road, but it still makes my skin crawl. I've gotten so used to being inside now, and any change in scenery feels like a step way out of my comfort zone. Wilda returns to the kitchen, ready for another box, and catches me on the doorstep, reluctant. Her face softens. She's been wearing a frown for days, but the sight of me is clearly so pitiful that her face almost melts into sadness.

"It's okay, Lori. You're safe. I promise."

When I don't respond, she holds out a hand to me. I shift the box I'm holding under my arm and hold her hand. She watches me expectantly as I step down, my legs shaking a little. We take it step by step. It's slow progress. But we come around the side of the house and I see the stall all set up. It's still dark, a proper winter morning. It's cold, and the only light comes from a streetlamp behind the garden bushes. Now that I've made the first steps, the garden doesn't seem so scary, but there's darkness everywhere, and it makes me uneasy. Wilda lets go of my hand so that I can set down my first box.

"It's okay," she says quietly. "The sun will be up soon. It's forecast to be a beautiful day."

I straighten up, my hands restless without a box to hold. I know I need to broach a difficult topic, but my nerves don't want to allow it. But I tell myself if I can brave the garden, I can brave this.

"Aunt Wilda…we never talked about what happened. In the attic."

Wilda doesn't seem surprised that I've brought it up. She offers her hand to me again and I take it as she leads me back indoors. "I shouldn't have reacted the way I did, Lori. I'm sorry if you felt shut out. There's really no need to talk about it."

"But…but it's important. The things that happened to you…"

"Some things are better forgotten, Lori. That's why I kept those things up there. I don't like to dwell on the past."

"I…I just thought maybe you'd like to talk to somebody about it all."

Wilda's eyes widen. "Lori…you're still a child. I couldn't possibly talk to you about these things."

"Why not? We're family. We're supposed to support one another."

Wilda looks surprised. We've made it back to the kitchen. She passes me another box, grabbing her own and turning her back on me. I don't think she wants me to see her face.

"You have enough on your plate, darling. Don't worry yourself about me. It was a long time ago."

I stop in the yard, watching her shuffle to the patch of grass. When she returns, she looks a little exasperated.

"Lori. I know you're trying to help-"

"You are the only person who could ever understand what I've lost," I blurt. Wilda seems bewildered.

"Darling…we've all lost someone."

"But you've not just lost one person. You…you've lost everyone. Like me."

Wilda's mouth hangs open. For a moment, I think I've said too much. But then she reaches out to set my box aside and hugs me hard.

"You haven't lost everyone. Neither have I," she whispers. "We have each other. We have our family. I know it hasn't always been that way…but I won't leave you." She pulls away from me, her hands resting on my shoulders. It's a gesture I'm familiar with. Rita used to do it before she told me something important.

"Life is full of loss. It's a harsh reality, and it can be hard to swallow. You and I know that better than most. But it's also full of surprises." Wilda's hands squeeze my shoulders. "I never knew I'd get to spend so much time getting to know my nieces. I don't care how long I've known you. You have brought light to my life that I thought I had lost forever. You and the girls. I don't need to talk about what I've lost any more. Of course, it's sad. Horribly sad. And it hurts me every single day. But I think it's better that I try and focus on what I've gained instead. That's what keeps me going."

I don't know what to say. My eyes are hot with tears. Wilda produces a tissue from her pocket and wipes my face.

"No more tears, Lori. More smiles. That's what our Rita would've wanted, isn't it?"

I sniffle, my throat tight. "I wish she was here. I wish…I wish she could see us all now."

Wilda kisses the top of my head gently. "I know. I hope somewhere, somehow, she can."

I've never been part of a garden sale before, but midday arrives, and I suspect ours is going pretty well. Honey and Rowena are yet to show up, but it feels like we've had all the neighbours on the street in to browse through all the bric-a-brac. There are several boxes of Marigold's clothes and trinkets on the lawn and they seem to be very popular. One woman spent a while rooting through one of her boxes before opting just to buy the whole thing. Over half of the boxes are almost empty, and Wilda looks pleased when we get a quiet moment to count up what we've made so far.

"This is good stuff! What should we do with the money, Lori?"

I shrug, not wanting to suggest anything. It's Wilda's money, after all. "Maybe a donation to charity?"

"You're a sweet kid," Wilda says, her smile almost reaching her tired eyes. She hands me a twenty note. 'Here. For my little helper.'

"I shouldn't…"

"Lori, it's okay. If you don't want to keep it, buy something for Vanessa. Her birthday is coming up. It can go towards a gift from us." Wilda looks up when she hears the gate clatter and smiles. "Speak of the Devil."

"And she shall show up fashionably late," Vanessa quips. I can't help grinning at the sight of her. She's wrapped up in a pink turtleneck jumper with patterned trousers that trail on the wet grass as she walks. Her hips sway as she walks, like this entire garden is her catwalk. She's stunning, and she's mine. She skips over to throw her arms around me before catching me off guard with a peck on the lips. I blush. I haven't told anyone about my day in the basement with Vanessa. Wilda seems unfazed, though. She simply smiles, slipping the money she was sorting through back into the safe box.

"Keep an eye on things, will you girls? I'm going to get Honey and Rowena out of their pits."

"Say no more. We've got this covered,' Vanessa promises. As Wilda leaves, Vanessa turns her attention back to me."

"Hey. Things seem good between you two."

I nod, leaning into her shoulder. 'Yeah. We talked this morning. It was nice."

"That's great," she says, pecking my lips again. I blush.

"I can't get used to you doing that."

"Oh my God. Is it bad? Do I slobber? Am I a bad kisser? Does my breath smell? Don't tell me I've been doing it wrong all these years."

I laugh. "I wouldn't know. You're my first kiss. But it seems okay to me."

"Just okay? Pfft. You really know how to butter a girl up."

I get brave and grab her by the hips, pulling her in for a kiss. Vanessa laughs against my lips.

"Are you trying to shut me up?"

"Nope. I'm not about to attempt the impossible."

Vanessa laughs again. Every time she giggles it warms my heart. Our noses bump, her arm slung around the back of my neck. We kiss again and I forget for a second that we're in my back garden, supposedly maintaining a stall.

"Gross!"

We break apart and see Rowena scowling by the side door, her hair dishevelled in comparison to its usual pin-straight style. Wilda and Honey follow her out and Wilda guides an unwilling Rowena by her elbow to the stall.

"I knew there was a reason I didn't want to come outside. I don't want to see Lori making out with anyone," Rowena grumbles.

"Well, if I'd known that was about to happen, I might have waited a few minutes longer," Wilda says, hiding a smile behind her hand.

"Wilda, it's so cold. Do we really have to stand out here?"

"Yes, Ro. It's good for you to get some fresh air now and then. If you're cold, put a scarf on."

"But it's, like, winter. You're supposed to stay inside."

"You should get twenty minutes of direct sunlight every day," Honey chips in with an accompanying yawn. "Don't fight it, Ro. Some sun will do you good. You're so pale."

"I like being pale. It's ghostly."

Wilda ruffles Rowena's hair, earning a scowl from her. "If you help me out for half an hour, you can have the first pick of the movie tonight. How about that?"

Rowena fixes her face almost instantly. "Star Wars. Oooh, or Ratatouille!"

"Don't decide just yet. You have to survive half an hour with me first."

Rowena's lips twitch into something that might be a smile, and her eyes are bright as she looks up at Wilda. I think this could be the fondest moment they've shared. Rowena and Honey position themselves behind the table and Vanessa grabs my hand.

"Looks like they've got the stall covered. Shall we go somewhere?"

I swallow. The word 'somewhere' hangs heavy in the air. I know what she's trying to do. Her eyes have lit up, sparked with possibility.

"Like…inside?"

Vanessa's still smiling but she seems a little nervous. "Well I thought since…I thought maybe I could take you over the road to mine. I could show you around. You'd love my bedroom. It's not…it's not too far away."

Everything has fallen through in a matter of seconds. I catch Honey watching us, listening in. It seems to add to the pressure. I fight for words breathlessly. It's like being in space, with no oxygen to be found.

Vanessa's face falls. She recognises the panic in my face moments after it appears. She scrambles for something to say, gripping my hand hard.

"It's okay. It's fine, Lori, I'm sorry. We can stay here." She tries for a smile. "I'll do a photoshoot of my room. I can always send the pictures over to you."

I nod, trying to smile too, but I'm beginning to see the one flaw of me and V. She has a life out there that she wants to share with me, but my entire life is contained in the walls around this house. I feel like Rapunzel. I'm trapped in my tower, and my Princess keeps climbing through my window to see me, but I'm not ready yet to make the leap yet to the world outside the prison I've made for myself.

BEDROOM

It's one of those mornings where the cold seems to seep through every crack in the house and settle in your bones. I lie in bed for a long time, acknowledging that I'm cold, but doing nothing about it. I only slept for three hours last night, and the tiredness is so heavy on me that I can't find the will to get up until Honey's alarm clock shudders on the bedside table. I listen to her sigh, her bed creaking as she gets up. I lie for a few more minutes before kicking the duvet off me as motivation to get up.

My morning routine is so sluggish that it seems to last for hours, but I'm still quick enough to get settled on the window sill before Vanessa leaves the house. I've got in the habit of sitting on the window bench with a book until Vanessa heads off to college. That way, I get to see her in the mornings. It's not as comfortable a nook as my alcove is, but there's something dreamy about being sat so close to the window. It makes me feel as though I'm almost outside, but still connected to the comforting inside of the house. This morning, frost laces itself on the corners of the glass and I can feel how cool it is if I press my palm against the window. My hand comes away damp with condensation. The start of February is here, and with it, the promise of snow.

It almost makes me miss being outside. Most years, we don't have much snow, and it dissolves quickly into a grey slush. But last year, the snow was beautiful. It was so thick that we couldn't even see strands of grass peeping through the white. Honey, Ro and I headed to the quarry together with baking trays to slide down the hills. There was no one else there and it felt like a winter wonderland dream, playing out in the cold until our hands turned numb. If it snows this year, the young kids on the street will probably have snowball fights, their gloved hands trying to pack powdery snow together with stiff fingers. I'll probably watch from the window and wish I was out there too. If I was well, maybe I'd head out with Ro and Honey to find another quarry. We could take Vanessa with us, and go for hot chocolate at Rococo's afterwards to warm us up. But I know it's not going to happen. My hand has turned numb on the window, and I let it slide away, knowing that's the closest to snow I'll get this year.

Vanessa leaves her house late today, as always. She's wrapped up in a puffer coat and her fur boots. She slips a little as she totters down her driveway, grinning to herself at her own clumsiness. She looks up and sees me, waving a little stiffly in her big coat. I wave back, resting my face against the window. Vanessa makes it to the end of her driveway with some difficulty and then blows me a kiss as she heads down the road.

It's hard watching her leave. I wish I had the confidence to chase her down the road in my pyjamas. I imagine slipping and sliding as I run to her, calling her name. I imagine we'd crash together like they always seem to in the movies, and our lips would crash too because we're just that happy to see each other. I'd kiss her until her frozen lips turned warm. And then we'd walk hand in hand to the bus stop. We'd jog to keep up with the bus as it moves off without us, laughing and sliding precariously. Isn't that what normal couples do? I bet not many people watch their girlfriend from their bedroom window, envying their ability to simply go out into the real world and have a normal life.

Looking out of the window becomes too much. I crawl back into bed and bury my face under the duvet. I doubt I'll come out for the rest of the day.

I wake to the sound of an email arriving on my phone. I check it groggily, my heart skipping a beat when I realise that it's Mrs Wickham.

Lori,

I haven't heard from you all week. If you're not interested in my guidance, then by all means continue to neglect deadlines, but if that's not the case, please reply pronto with something spectacular! I'm sure you've created something fabulous this week, but I can't pass you on this module if you don't send it to me. If something is happening, please let me know so I can try and help out.

Kind (if slightly impatient) regards, Mrs Wickham.

I feel sick to my stomach. I haven't written anything since Marigold left two weeks ago. I've been desperate to. It's usually the only escape I have. But after days of not sleeping, and wearily ploughing through the rest of my work, my Creative Writing work has been pushed further and further back on my list of priorities. I sink my head into my hands. I can't exactly tell Mrs Wickham

I've not done the work. I could risk humiliating myself and telling her that I'm falling apart – I'm not sleeping, my Mum is on the other side of the world, and my girlfriend seems to be living life for the both of us. But I can't do that.

I grab my laptop hastily, checking the time. I've been asleep for hours. Grogginess clouds my head, but I know I have to produce something, and fast. My hands are shaking as a dark tale unfolds beneath my fingers about a girl who gets trapped in her own nightmares. It's full of horrible mistakes and clichés and repetition, but I can barely bear to read back over the first paragraph. I type a half-hearted apology, dubbing the piece a 'work in progress' and send the story off, knowing full well it's the worst piece of fiction I've ever written.

I spend half the afternoon curled up in bed, thinking about my sloppy piece of work. I wonder how Mrs Wickham will respond to it. Right now, I'm too tired to care much about whether she likes it or not, but I know whatever she thinks will probably bother me. I know I should get out of bed and think about starting my history coursework, but there's no one home to tell me to get up, and so I don't. I tell myself it's just one of those kinds of days, but come to think of it, I've felt like doing this for weeks now. I close my eyes to fight off the headache from my last nap, hoping that someone will get home soon to distract me from my own thoughts.

Rowena and Wilda arrive home at the same time and I pull on some jogging pants, not wanting to look like I've spent the entire day in bed. Rowena pops her head around the door, grinning.

"Wanna come play with Hammy for a while?"

I pull myself off my bed, my joints a little stiff. "Sure."

"And will you help me with my history project? I think you did something similar when you were in my year."

I stifle a yawn. "Mhmm."

Rowena doesn't seem to notice how weary I am. She chatters to me as she gets Hammy out of his cage and lets him run around on her bed. She laughs when he clambers onto my legs and up my sleeve. It's cute, but I'm so tired that even laughing seems like a lot of effort. When I hear Honey come back from college, I'm almost relieved to have a respite from Rowena's chatter. She looks surprised to find Rowena's bedroom door wide open and she pops her head around.

"What are you guys doing?"

"We're playing with Hammy! You wanna come in?"

Honey looks like she might say yes. Her mouth opens and she almost speaks. Then she presses her lips closed and smiles.

"I can't. I have work to do."

Rowena shrugs, scooping Hammy up and nuzzling him with her nose. Honey lingers for a few moments by the door, her toes edging the space between the landing and Rowena's room. Then she turns around and heads into our bedroom.

After dinner, Honey disappears upstairs, and I reluctantly follow her soon after. I know by now Mrs Wickham will have replied to my email. Honey is sitting at the desk when I enter our room, sipping black coffee. She winces at the taste and then lowers her head back to her textbook, scanning a page. I try to be quiet as I sit down and open my laptop. A pang of fear hits me as I see Mrs Wickham's email staring me in the face. I click on it and fidget as it loads.

Dear Lori,

Thank you for getting back to me. It's not your strongest piece in terms of style – I can sense that you might have rushed it a little. You can find notes attached as usual, and I expect another piece next Monday. I know you're under a lot of stress at the moment with your home life and your other subjects, but you have a lot of talent and I'd hate to see you waste it.

I noticed this piece is very different from your usual work, and if you don't mind me saying, it's rather dark. If you aren't feeling yourself, you can reach out to me. If I came across harshly in my previous email, please disregard it. I am here for all of my students if they need to talk, and since we don't see each other in person, I'd like to reiterate that fact to you. I would hate to see any of my writing family suffering. I hope I'm wrong and that I've contacted you on an off week, but I just wanted to make sure.

Mrs Wickham.

I can't quite believe what I'm reading. How did Mrs Wickham manage to suss my entire state of mind from a poorly written short story? I put my head in my hands, sighing. She's right, of course. I'm a mess, and my work is suffering because of it. But she can't know that. No one can. I need to hold myself together. If Marigold read this email, she'd be packing me back off to college right away, and that won't help anything. Right now, I can't handle that. I'm not sure when I'll ever be able to handle it again, let alone now. I close my laptop and sit away from it. I need to get away. But there's nowhere to go. Not when I can't go out there.

I open the window for a while, trying to control my breathing. It helps. The air's a little warmer than this morning, but it still has bite. I close my eyes and let it refresh my face.

"Lori?"

I turn around. Honey is standing by her desk, a textbook clutched close to her chest. She blinks several times in succession, like she's adjusting to a bright light. Seeing her face fully surprises me. She looks awful. Like Marigold, her face is thinner. Her hair is tight in its ponytail, piled messily at the top of her scalp. Her lips are chapped and her eyes have dark circles beneath them. It strikes me as odd that I haven't noticed this before, but I've been in a world of my own. Now that I've noticed, though, it's impossible not to think about it.

"Could you run through some test questions with me? I'm lagging a bit."

I nod. "Of course I can…"

Honey sits opposite me on her own bed. This is something we've done together a thousand times and I'm used to it by now. But her twitchiness is worrying me a little. If she's noticed my concern, she doesn't let on.

"What chapter?"

"Seven. Algebra. I'll work them out on my pad and you can check them. Then I'm not tempted to check the answers."

I doubt Honey would ever cheat, but I agree anyway. I read out a complicated looking equation, filled with random looking letters and numbers. Honey nods to herself as she notes the equation down. I watch her attempt to solve it, her pen hovering over the page and her tongue stuck out the side of her mouth. She scans over it several times. Her forehead wrinkles. Her eyes droop. She sighs, gesturing at the desk.

"Is my coffee over on the table?"

I glance over. There are four mugs resting on top of various textbooks and pads of paper.

"Are those all from today?"

"I'm thirsty."

"You've only been home a few hours. It's late, Honey. You'll never sleep if you have another coffee. Don't you think-"

"What's with the lecture?" Honey snaps. She rolls her eyes, standing up. "It's okay. I'll get it myself."

She grabs the cup and returns to her equation. Her face returns to its frowning state. I watch her hand. Her wrist is trembling. She sniffs and readjusts her position. She sips coffee. Shuffles again. She blinks a few times, her eyelids fluttering. Her hands paw at her eyes. I chew my thumb, not knowing what to do. Now that I've noticed how twitchy she is, it's hard to ignore.

"Maybe you should just try again in the morning. You can't just keep drinking coffee."

Honey shakes her head, putting down her pen to rub her hands together. They're strangely pale. They're so pale, they almost look blue. "I'm fine."

"You don't look so good."

"Wow, thanks. You don't look your best either, Lori, if we're swapping insults."

I back off. It's not often Honey is in this bad of a mood. In the corner of my eye, I can see her fidgeting, making zero progress on her equation. I pretend to be interested in something on my laptop, but I can't stop watching Honey. She shakes her head to herself, standing up.

"I'll finish up in Marigold's room. Less distractions," she says, more to herself than to me. She drifts from the room, muttering the equation to herself. Her rucksack is still on her bed as she leaves the room. I'm suddenly curious whether she's having this much trouble with her other subjects. I know I shouldn't snoop, but I'm worried about her. I want to know what's going on.

I open her bag. It's somehow still meticulously neat, her papers all contained in clear plastic folders that aren't even bent in the corners. That's why the small tin in the bottom of her bag stands out so much. Checking Honey hasn't returned, I take out the box.

It's an old mint tin, but something tells me she doesn't keep sweets in there. When I crack it open, I see it's filled with an assortment of orange pills. Some are round, others are capsules. I rattle one out into my hand and smell it. It's not a vitamin. Then I spot a piece of paper beneath the pills. I pull it out. My eyes float over the words *amphetamine* and *inhibitor*. I rush through to the symptoms. Mood changes. Weight loss. Headaches. Sleep deficiency. All symptoms that fit Honey. I wonder how many of these she's taking a day. It can't be a good amount – the box is half empty. Still unsure what drug I'm looking at, I type in the brand on the internet. When I see, I finally understand what Honey's up to. I grab the tin and storm to Marigold's room. I have to talk to her.

Honey looks up in surprise as I enter the room. I hold the tin up, gritting my teeth.

"Really, Honey? Study drugs?"

Honey's eyes widen and she shushes me. She stands up and races to shut the door behind me.

"You went through my bag?"

"I had to. I had to know what's going on with you."

"I'm fine, Lori. I didn't tell you because I knew you'd worry. I'm just getting something to help me along with my studies."

"Have you read the health warnings on these things? And these are prescription drugs. How the hell did you get these? They're used for narcolepsy and ADHD. You don't have either of those things."

"I know someone who gets them for me, okay? It's not a big deal. Everyone at college uses them."

"That doesn't mean you should too."

"Lori, I swear, you're making a fuss."

"Have you seen yourself lately? You're a mess."

Honey's lips tighten. "That makes two of us. How about this? If I stop taking these, you'll come back to college. Right? Seeing as you know what's best for everyone, including yourself."

"That's…that's different. I'm just trying to help! I'm worried about you."

"Well don't be. Focus on yourself. God knows you've got enough on your plate. Don't think I don't know what a state you're in. You're having nightmares again. You walk around like a zombie. So I don't know why you're bothering to come in here and lecture me about my health. I've always stayed out of your sorry business, so maybe you should stay out of mine.'"

"But-"

"Don't tell anyone about this. I mean it. I'll never forgive you for it," Honey snarls. I swallow hard, my back pressed against the door. She's never threatened me before. It's not in her nature. I know it must be these pills throwing her off. Sure enough, she catches herself and her eyes soften a little.

"Please, Lori? Don't ruin this for me."

"Ruin things? Really?"

"Lori…"

She doesn't want me telling her how to live her life. Just like I don't want her to tell me how to live mine.

But right now, watching her self-sabotage is too hard. I grab the door handle, and wipe my face of emotion.

"I won't say anything for now. I'll give you some time to think this over…but please, Honey…don't carry on doing this. You're making yourself sick. You're smarter than this."

Honey folds her arms and juts out her chin. "I'm building my future. There's nothing stupid about that."

I swallow. It seems like there's no getting through to her. I close the door behind me, shutting my sister in the room. Because she's right. I can't even look after myself. Trying to save her too is like saving someone from drowning when you've already sank to the bottom of the ocean.

VANESSA'S ROOM

"Look, Lori, you'll like this bit the best! Look at my poster!"

I maintain a smile as Vanessa shows me around her bedroom via FaceTime. She's grinning as she moves the camera to show herself with a Chocolat poster behind her. It's clearly very old and frayed at the edges. After all, the movie came out years ago. But it does make me love her even more.

"It's the perfect centrepiece."

"Right? I knew you'd like it. It's the most important part of my entire room." She flops down onto her bed with a satisfied sigh. "It's cute, right?"

"It's great," I tell her, my cheeks hurting from holding up my smile. It's not a lie that I'm telling her, but I'm having a hard time with this call. It only serves as a reminder that I can't see her room in person. That I'm too scared to simply cross the road and be there with her. It's not even far away, but my anxiety keeps me rooted right here in the window seat. If I look out, I can

207

see Vanessa's room from here. How hard can it be to just walk over there right now?

Near impossible, I remind myself.

"Lori…don't drift away on me," Vanessa says softly. "And stop worrying about it. You'll make it here someday."

I swallow. "Do you think so?"

"I know so. I know you want to. So you will. I can't pretend to understand how you feel, Lori, but I know nothing bad lasts forever."

I smile wearily. It's tempting to believe her, but then again, I've found that life tends to throw everything at some people and nothing at others. Vanessa and I couldn't be more opposite. She's grown up in a typical family, in an ordinary house surrounded by people with normal lives. My life has felt like a constant race, always trying to outrun one problem or another. And now that I'm standing still, hiding away in this house, it's beginning to feel like my problems might be catching up. Like they're gathering outside this window, just waiting for me to be brave enough to face them.

It makes me want to never let my guard down again.

"Hey, Lori…there's something I've been meaning to talk to you about for a while. If that's okay?"

I frown. I've never heard Vanessa sound so uncertain. My heart skips a beat. What is this about? Why has she waited to do this over FaceTime? Why couldn't she say this in person? My imagination is running wild. I swallow back my fear.

"Of course that's okay. What's on your mind?"

Vanessa takes a deep breath and smiles. "Well…I applied for this thing a few weeks ago. I thought it would be no big deal, that I wouldn't hear back, that it wouldn't come to anything in the scheme of things…but I heard back a few days ago. Basically, I applied to this course in New York…it's like a bunch of writing classes and meeting other writers…it lasts two weeks and it's fully paid for if you get a scholarship, which is what I applied for…and they accepted me! I could barely believe it, Lori. I never thought I'd be accepted in a million years!"

"That's incredible, Vanessa! I'm so proud of you. Of course they accepted you. They'd be stupid not to," I exclaim. She giggles, her face split by her smile.

"I'm still in shock! I wasn't expecting it at all." She pauses, her smile slipping a little. "But the thing is…if I go…"

"What do you mean *if?* Of course you're going!"

"But Lori…if I go, I leave on Friday. It would mean…well, it would mean leaving you."

I stare at my screen in disbelief. I can't believe she's willing to consider rejecting the opportunity of a lifetime just to be closer to me. I shake my head.

"Vanessa…please don't be ridiculous. You're going, end of story."

Vanessa's expression droops. "But…but I'm worried about you, Lori. I just…you haven't been yourself lately. I know you're struggling with Mari being away. And I just…well, I would feel terrible leaving you beh-"

"No, Vanessa. We don't do this," I tell her firmly. "Listen to me…I care about you way too much to ever hold you back from anything. If the shoe was on the other foot, I know you'd say the same thing. It's two weeks. The opportunity of a lifetime. You deserve it more than anything. And listen to me properly now…I know you want to help. I know you think you can make things better for me if you just try hard enough. But that's not how life works. I have to figure this out myself."

"But-"

"Vanessa, please. Just this once, let me speak. You're my girlfriend. You're not my carer. It's not your job to look after me, and you're certainly not putting your life on hold for me. You're going to go to New York. You're going to have an amazing time and send me photographs and eat good food and see the sights. That's what I want for you. Don't make something that's totally about you about me. I won't have it."

Vanessa sighs, her eyes filled with tears. I've never seen her so upset before. I want to hold her, and suddenly the screen between us makes it feel like we're a thousand miles apart. Soon we will be, I suppose. Selfishly, I wish she'd stay with me. But my lifestyle makes me feel selfish all the time. I refuse to do it this time.

"I pictured the two of us going together some day," Vanessa murmured. "If only you could come with me…I know you would've got accepted to the programme too, if you'd applied. But…but I know that's out of the question."

I nod. "For now. But maybe someday. This time, though…this is a golden opportunity for you. And I'll be waiting to hear all about it. I can live through you."

Vanessa nods, but she still looks so sad that it makes my throat tighten. I force a big smile for her. I don't want to give her any doubts about leaving.

"You'd better bring me one of those I heart NY t-shirts back from Times Square, that's all I'm saying."

Vanessa laughs, wiping at her eyes. "I will. I promise. Are you sure about this?"

"Vanessa…don't ask again. Of course I am."

But I'm not. Because an hour later when we hang up the call, I begin to realise what Vanessa's absence will feel like. She's been keeping me going for so long. While Marigold has been away, she's been the only one I've spoken to much, other than Wilda. Honey is withdrawn from me and Rowena is the same as always, locked away in her room away from the world. I tell myself that I'll be fine. That my declining mood these past few weeks can't get much worse.

But I know from experience how that's not true.

BATHROOM

You never know rock bottom until you sink that low. But I'm there now. I lie beneath my duvet in the middle of the day, the grey winter sky doing nothing for my mood. I spend my days alone while Wilda is out at work and my sisters are studying. Now, I don't even have Vanessa passing my window each morning to lift my mood. I wanted her to go, and I don't regret telling her to. But now that she's left, nothing can seem to get me out of bed in the morning.

Mostly, though, I feel the absence of my mothers. Rita not being here has been hard for months, but now that Marigold is gone too, it's like someone is constantly pummeling me in the stomach. I wait to hear from her beneath the covers. If she called, maybe I'd tell her how bad things feel. The night terrors, the loneliness, the hatred I feel for myself for not being able to lead a normal life.

But it's been a week since I last heard from her.

No one seems to be acknowledging how bad things have gotten here. Rowena spends most of her time locked away in her room. Honey is in such a daze that she floats around the house like a ghost. She's barely speaking to me anyway, but she's quieter than she's ever been. Wilda is trying her best with us all. She tries to get through to Rowena, but she just keeps shutting her out. She's been trying to get Honey to eat properly and to take study breaks, but Honey's presence has become like a curse around here, dark and depressing. And of course, Wilda spends a lot of her time focussed on me, trying to get me to shower and brush my hair and take care of myself, but it's like I've forgotten how.

Sometimes, I lie for hours, stomach cramping with hunger, bladder busting, my mouth dry with dehydration, and I can't bring myself to do anything about it. I have no desire to participate in life at this moment in time. I wish it would pass. I've felt this way before and it got better, eventually. But there's nothing to lift my mood any more. I search for signs of love around me, but it feels so far out of reach. So I just lie here and fester beneath the sheets. I don't answer my texts from Vanessa, though I know I should. I don't bother with my college work. I stop trying to lift myself out of this negative space.

And it consumes me.

Sometimes when I feel like this, it helps a little to close my eyes and picture Rita talking to me. In my mind, we're sitting on our old sofa back home, the smell of lavender filling the air and the calming purple walls nestling us inside. I listen to her tell me over and over that after everything I've been through, it's normal for life to feel tough sometimes.

But a few days ago, when I was getting lost in the false memory, I noticed something that broke down the last of my resolve. In my mind, where I hold her so sacred, where I keep her alive in my thoughts, I forgot the sound of her voice.

It was just for a split second, but something in the way I remembered her was off. The husk of her voice wasn't there, her pitch too high, her words flat and cold. And it terrified me so much that I retreated straight back to the real world, tears falling down my cheeks.

Because nothing terrifies me more than remembering that she's gone. Nothing hurts more than waking up in the morning and knowing I won't see her, won't hear her voice, won't smell her perfume. And now, I can't even seem to keep her alive inside my head. When I lose her there, I feel as though I'll lose everything I have left.

I bury my face in my pillow. I have no idea what time it is, but I've been here since I woke up. I don't know if I can face getting out of bed at all today. At least it'll just be me and Wilda in the house. Rowena is going out with some friends and Honey is at a study sleepover. I miss talking to Honey, but she's got issues of her own. I can't take on hers and she can't take on mine. So we're just both suffering in silence, shutting one another out, hoping it'll go away.

But it's starting to feel like it won't.

Time passes. I hear Wilda's car pulling up outside and I still don't stir. I know as soon as she enters the house that she wants to come and check on me, but she waits a while. By the time I hear her softly knocking on my bedroom door, I'm too exhausted to even answer her. After a while, she comes in anyway.

"Lori…Lori darling, can you roll over so I can see you?"

It takes a lot of effort, but I manage it. Wilda has a desperate look in her eyes as she surveys me. She swallows.

"It's just the two of us tonight. I bought a bunch of your favourite snacks. I thought maybe we could go downstairs, watch a movie."

I close my eyes. I don't know how to tell her that the energy it would take to do something like that might end me entirely. "I don't think I can tonight."

"Lori…I think you need to. I think it's necessary."

I open my eyes again, guilt stabbing at my chest. I feel cruel for putting her through this. She never asked to inherit this family and all of its problems. I can see that she doesn't know what to do with me, how to cope.

"I'm sorry, Wilda," I whisper, my throat dry. "But I can't. I'm too…I'm too tired."

Her lip wobbles and she reaches out to cup my cheek. "You're wasting away on me, sweetheart. I…I don't know what to do. Do you need to see a doctor?"

My throat is so tight that it feels impossible to speak.

"I don't know," I croak. "There's…there's something wrong with me."

"Oh Lori."

I put my head in my hands, soft sobs wracking my body. "I just…I just don't feel like I can take it anymore. I don't know what to do. My heart…it hasn't felt whole in so long. I feel like I'm giving up and I don't know how to stop it."

Wilda wraps her arms around me and I lean into her chest, crying so hard that it hurts. I cling to her hard, keeping myself grounded. I don't want to slip away, but it feels like I might. How did it get like this? How did I become this person? I weep so hard that it feels like there's a knife slicing through my chest.

"Please don't give up, Lori," Wilda whispers into my hair. "I know I'm no replacement for my sister...no one ever could be. But I love you. We all do. And seeing you like this is killing me. I'm sorry I'm not better equipped...I never...I never thought I'd get to be a mother. But I'm here for you. I want to look after you."

My head rests heavy on her shoulder. I've come to love Aunt Wilda too. And not just because I have to, not just because she's an extension of our family. She's right. She's been the closest thing to a mother I've had these past few weeks. I'm not about to turn her love away just because she's not the one who adopted me.

"I don't want to scare you," I whisper. "I'm sorry. I just...I've hit a new low. I can't picture where my life is heading. Every day, the pain feels worse. I thought...I thought I would finally get my shot at happiness...and now Rita's gone. And I think about how she'll never see me graduate, or get married, or adopt kids of my own. And I just...I think it all just seems so pointless without her."

"I know," Wilda says, pulling back and cupping my cheeks. Her eyes are swimming with tears. "I think we all lost a piece of ourselves the day Rita died. We weren't close in recent years...but I missed her terribly. And my biggest regret will always be not reconnecting with her properly. But we were so, so lucky to have her. Even if only for a time. We don't get to keep everything forever. But we were the lucky ones. And that's why it hurts so much that she's gone. But it doesn't mean you don't get to live a life. She would hate to see you this way." Wilda swallows. "I know everything feels impossible right now. For a while...I was like you. After I lost my babies...I didn't know how to function. And then my husband left me. I lay alone in this house and thought that I would never be whole again."

My eyes sting with tears. "Wilda…"

"There's a light at the end of it all, I promise you. It takes time. It takes courage. But I know if I can do it, you can too. I was alone then. But you're not alone now. I'll never allow that again. No matter what…you'll always have me."

I look at Wilda now and I see RIta in her eyes. The strength of her, the loyalty of her, the endless love inside her. I've spent so long seeing the differences between Rita and Wilda, but at their core, I know they're the same. And it hurts to look at Wilda now, to see how similar they truly are. But she's right. As long as I have Wilda, I'm not alone.

As long as Wilda is with me, Rita is too.

"Thank you," I whisper. I don't have much left inside me to give, but right now, whatever's left, I want to give it to her. Wilda is the one person who has stuck by me from the moment we showed up in this house. She's the lifeline I didn't know I needed. And she's trying so hard.

"You don't ever need to thank me, Lori. This is what family is for," Wilda says gently. "Do you think you can manage a bath? I can run one for you. I can change your sheets and get you some fresh pyjamas…sometimes the little things, they can help."

I don't know how to tell her that it probably won't help. I've spent years watching influencers on social media preaching how a bubble bath and a face mask is enough self care to get you through anything. But I don't want to let her down. I want to try. I nod slowly. Wilda cracks a sad smile.

"Alright, darling. You wait there."

I close my eyes a while longer as I hear the sound of the taps running. When Wilda returns, she helps me up out of the bed. I feel embarrassed at how stiff my body has become, at how hard it seems to do the most basic things. It feels like my body has aged thirty years. I'm so weak that I can barely stand. But Wilda helps me to the bathroom. She's lit some candles for me and put plenty of bubble bath in the basin. She plants a kiss on my head and the warmth it gives me makes me want to cry. I feel starved of it. It nourishes me just enough to get the strength to undress and get in the bath. I lie in the water for a long time while Wilda changes the bed. I cry a little. I feel the aches leaving my bones. I slowly wash days worth of grime from my body. By the time I get out of the bath, my legs shaking a little, I feel clean, at least.

I change into fresh pyjamas and head back to my room, hair dripping. I'm exhausted enough now that I just want to collapse back into bed, but I stand a little taller for Wilda's sake. She's made the bed and opened the window, letting some fresh air inside. It's cold, but it feels easier to breathe in here now. She's waiting with a hairbrush.

"Come here, darling. Let me get some of the tangles out of your hair."

I sit on the bed and allow her to gently brush through my matted hair. She takes it slow, trying not to tug at the toughest knots on my head. I close my eyes. I don't ever recall someone brushing my hair for me before. Never as a child, certainly. It feels nice, even when the brush pulls. The ritual takes a long time, given the state of my hair, but by the time it's done, I feel somewhere close to human again.

It's not enough. But it's a start.

OUTSIDE

Somewhere along the way, sadness starts to feel more like anger.

It's been four days since Wilda and I spoke and she convinced me to push a little harder. We've kept the conversation between us, which I'm glad of. I don't want anyone else knowing just how hard I hit rock bottom. But now, as I'm coming up for air, it's not the ache of sadness trying to push me back under.

It's this hot rage inside me. It's not a feeling I have often, and the burn of it is almost too much to bear. I'm angry with myself for getting so low, even if it feels like it's out of my control. I'm angry that Marigold is nowhere to be seen, that she's so out of touch with my life that I don't trust her any longer. I'm furious that someone took Rita away from me, the person who made my life worth living in the first place.

And I don't think of the good times now. I think about how much I hate the fact that Rita's left us all broken this way. She was the catalyst for Rowena shutting us out, for Honey losing herself, for Marigold abandoning us in our time of need. I hate that I let Rita become my lifeline. I hate that all the progress I made fell apart when she died. I hate that I'm so reliant. I hate that I never stood a chance in this life.

I feel this urge to scream out the window into this quiet, neat neighbourhood. I want to disrupt this place a little, because it feels way too good to be true. Out there looks so safe, and yet it scares me half to death. And I'm tired of it. I just want to get back to the way things were. I was still scared before, but at least it was manageable. At least I had some hold on who I am.

Hot tears pour down my cheeks for hours of the day, but it does little to douse the fire burning inside me. When does it end, if ever?

My phone buzzes on the windowsill. I glance down to see who it is.

-I haven't heard from you in a while, Lori…is everything okay? Please talk to me. I got home two days ago and you've not messaged me back. I miss you.

I swallow hard. Vanessa. I've been avoiding her. Not because I don't want to see her, but because I don't want her to see *me*. I'm worse than I've ever been. I'm scared she can't handle me this way. I'm scared she'll lose interest when she realises just how deep my issues run. The anxious part of me, the dominant part of me, is telling me that she will never want someone who can't even muster the energy to look after herself. I haven't washed since Wilda ran me that bath the other day. I haven't eaten a proper meal in days, as much as Wilda has tried to feed me good food. I am a mess.

And now I'm angry with myself again.

I press my palms against the window pane and feel the coolness of it. It brings me down to Earth a little.

Lately, my old tricks haven't been working. I binge ate three packets of sour sweets to try and calm my anxiety and the sugar rush only made it worse. I used up all of the bubbles that Vanessa got for me and still my lungs struggle for air. I counted to ten so many times that it made me want to scream, and when I reached the last number, I didn't feel any better. And aromatherapy will never work for me again. Smelling lavender only brings me crashing back down to this reality where Rita is no longer here.

Some part of me knows it can't get better than this. Not while I'm trapped in here, the prison I locked myself in and threw away the key. I close my eyes. I need to change. I need to let myself live life again. Because the child in me still needs to experience the world, to see all the things that scare me with my own eyes. I'll never be an adventurer, or a jet-setter, or someone who grabs life by the reins…but there has to be more to life than this. I want to be someone who isn't scared to walk to the corner shop to buy milk when we run out. I want to be the person who crosses the road to see the girl she's falling in love with. I want to be someone who lives with their mental illnesses and isn't consumed by it. I'll never leave anxiety behind. I'll always know depression, and it'll never be easy to leave the house. I know that, deep in my heart.

But that doesn't mean I can't have good days.

I want today to be a good day.

My heart is beating so hard that I feel sick. My vision is blurred as anxiety takes over, but my feet carry me down the stairs to the front door. I grapple for the ten pound note on the sideboard and a set of keys. I'm breathing hard, locked in to these feelings until I tell myself to turn back. But I'm not going to do that. I can't do it to myself any longer. Every instinct inside me is telling me that if I go out there, I won't survive. Memories of Rita lying in the street come back to me in a tidal wave and I clutch my stomach, fighting nausea as curtains pull across my eyes. When my anxiety is at its worst, it's like I can't see. I'm panting now. This is the most exercise I've done in weeks, and I've only walked to the front door. If I keep pushing my body like this, I'm convinced I'll have a heart attack.

But I stumble on forward. I swing open the door to the porch and shove my feet inside a pair of shoes without looking at them. I don't even think they're mine. But it's too late to worry about that now, because I'm opening the porch door, feeling the winter air hit my face. It feels so strong that it's almost like it's shoving me back, telling me not to brave the outside world. That's what I tell myself.

But this has always been an internal battle. It's not me against the world - it's me against myself. The world may not have been kind to me, but it doesn't discriminate. It wounds us all from time to time. I know that, deep down.

I can't sit around and wait for the world to change.

I have to make a change in myself.

I'm crying hard as my feet find the doorstep. My hands grip the porch, the only part of me still inside the house. I can't imagine how I look now, but I don't care. This is my moment. I'm doing this for myself and no one else. I force myself to let go of the house. I haven't been out the front of this house in almost five months. Before I can let the anxiety win, I stagger out onto the driveway, onto the street.

It's like coming alive and dying all at once. The cold winter air fills my lungs and it's almost as though I'm blowing away cobwebs. All the while, my chest burns like I've just run a marathon and trying to breathe feels harder than ever. I stagger forward on legs that don't want to move, but I keep pushing. I'm terrified, my entire body shaking from head to toe. *This is wrong. Go back, go back, go back…*

But I can't stay there forever. This is the hardest thing I've ever had to do, but if I don't get out of here soon, I don't know what I'll do.

I've been stagnant for so long that I've forgotten what it feels like to move. To use my body, to appreciate what it can do. Before I know what I'm doing, I'm running. Away from the house, away from everything I know to be safe. I know if I don't push myself now, I might never have the courage again. I run with tears streaming down my cheeks. My body groans and ice bites at my cheeks, but I'm doing it. I don't know where I'm headed, blinded by the fear inside me, but all I know is I'm out.

I've made it out.

CAFE

Rococo's smells like coffee, and I can't stand coffee. But there's a warm cup cocooned in my hands, warming my numb fingers. I try to focus on that. I only have to wait a few more minutes. I've made it to the place Vanessa told me so much about. I managed to message her and tell her I'm here, though I'm so dazed that I barely remember how I got here. Now I only have to survive until she gets here. And then I can go home. I'll have done enough for one day.

I'm shivering, but I'm sweating. My armpits are damp. Do I smell? I know I must. I've sweated right through my pyjama top. I can't remember the last time I brushed my teeth, and they feel grimy as I run my tongue over them nervously. My breath must stink. I haven't even eaten much to dirty them, though. I haven't even sipped my hot chocolate yet. And that's what I came here for. For hot chocolate. For her. To prove I can.

The longer the wait, the more I want to give up on myself again. Vanessa said she'd get here as fast as she can. But that time frame could span from minutes to hours. How long will I be sitting here? I look around. People are staring. I can feel it. I'm in my pyjamas, for God's sake. It makes my skin crawl. There's more sweating. My heart feels like it's been force-fed three energy drinks.

"Lori, oh my God…what happened to you?"

I look up and see Vanessa staring at me from the door of the café. Her mouth hangs open and she quickly runs a hand through her hair. She looks around for a place where we can find refuge, before realising there's nowhere we can go. There's nowhere to hide. She stumbles to me and grabs my hand, pulling me to my feet.

"Come on. Let's get you out of here. I'll take you home. You're okay. You're safe with me, I promise."

I let her steer me. We clumsily bump our way through the door and out into the cold. I close my eyes and put my trust in her guidance. She moves slowly, like she's scared of pushing me too far, too fast.

Vanessa's hand falls to my waist, pulling me against her hip.

"You must be freezing, Lori. Why did you leave without getting dressed?"

My teeth chatter. "I…I wasn't thinking. I just…I didn't plan to leave the street. I didn't really plan to leave the house. And then…and then I did."

Vanessa blinks in disbelief. "Okay. Okay, well we'll get you home. It's not far. Look, we're halfway there."

I can't believe I made it this far alone. I've never even been into the town here, I should have got lost. I'm a little pleased with myself, but it's not enough to override the fear. Now that I'm back outside, I see opportunities for disaster everywhere. Cars rushing past. Builders working on unstable scaffolding. A woman operating a tractor turning into a road. I start to shiver, but Vanessa has a tight hold of me, and she's almost a good enough substitute for Rita.

I want to weep when I see our street coming into view. I bury my face into Vanessa's shoulder and she guides me back. I feel the familiarity of the world beginning to return. This house is all I know right now. It's all I want to know for a while. I can't see myself leaving the house again for a long, long time. But I've made progress. I know that much.

I almost slip as Vanessa helps me up the step, eager to get back inside. I kick my snow covered shoes off in the porch and open the door. Wilda is pacing the living room, chewing her thumb. She sees me and her face relaxes. She rushes to hug me, squeezing me tight.

"Oh God, Lori. I didn't know where you were. I was worried sick."

I bury my face in her hair, fighting off tears. "I'm sorry."

"The door was open, there was no sign of you…what were you thinking?"

"I'm sorry. I'm so sorry…"

Wilda shakes her head, her expression pained, but there's love in her eyes. She cups my cheeks.

"As long as you're safe. What happened?"

I pull away, wiping at my eyes. "I hardly know myself. I just…I had to get out for a while. But I'm…I'm so tired now. I can't do that again today."

Wilda manages a smile, brushing away my tears. There are tears in her own eyes, but right now, she looks so proud of me. "You're safe now. And you don't need to push yourself any further. You did so well. Let's take this as a small victory, hmm? Let's get you settled down…I'll put the kettle on. Hot chocolate?"

I'm still holding a Rococo's carton in my hands. The hot chocolate is cold and congealed inside. I shake my head. "I'm okay. I don't…I don't think I could face it right now."

"Okay, dear, but I'm making you a hot honey and lemon. You're freezing." Wilda looks at Vanessa. "Are you having a drink?"

"Hot chocolate, if it's not too much trouble."

Wilda nods and heads to the kitchen, leaving me alone with Vanessa. It's the first moment we've shared in weeks that isn't clouded by chaos. I hang my head.

"You don't have to stay. I'm sorry you have to see me like this. I shouldn't have-"

Vanessa takes my hands in hers. "Don't talk like that, Lori. I won't hear it. I'm not giving up on you. I'm not going anywhere."

We sit in silence for a while. It should be awkward, but it's not, somehow. It feels good to have her back at my side. When Wilda returns with the drinks, she looks concerned.

"Are you girls alright?"

Vanessa nods, catching my eye with a soft smile. "Yeah. I guess we just have some things to talk over."

"Say no more. I'll make myself scarce," Wilda says, backing out of the room. Vanessa turns to me, sitting cross-legged.

"So. I didn't hear from you the whole time I was away. Did I do something wrong?"

I close my eyes and shake my head. "No. Of course not."

"You know, if you needed some space, you could have just told me. I would have understood. I know you're having a hard time," she says. She doesn't sound angry, though she has every right to be. She sounds more concerned than anything. I press the heel of my hand to my temple.

"It wasn't you. I just...it's been a rough few weeks. Rougher than usual." I swallow hard. I know I need to be as truthful with her as possible, and that means admitting to how I've been feeling. "I haven't been out of bed in weeks. I've been eating a lot less. I...I haven't been thinking straight. Things have just felt...wrong. I've been miserable."

Vanessa squeezes my hand harder. "Lori...you could've told me. I would've come home. I would have made sure you were okay."

"I think part of me knew that, and I didn't want it. I didn't want to hold you back."

"You have to stop acting like you're a burden. You're not."

"I am. I know I am. And I don't want to be. I just want to be normal."

Vanessa smiles sadly. "Normal is hard to come by, Lori. Everyone has their issues. I know you, sweetie. I know who you are, and this comes with the package. That might not be okay with you, but it's okay with me until you're healed. That'll take time. Longer than a day. I know what you did today was progress...but it'll take longer than this for you to be better."

"I...I know."

"So stop being so hard on yourself. And stop shutting me out. I want to be with you. I want to stick by you even when times are tough." She manages to catch my eye, even though I'm avoiding looking directly at her. "Do you hear what I'm saying? I'm never going to give up on you. No matter how things pan out in our lives...I'm always going to care about you. I'm always going to be your friend, first and foremost."

She presses a kiss to my forehead and I feel a lump forming in my throat. She holds me gently for a long time and I grip her back. I've missed her an impossible amount. She peppers kisses on my cheeks, her arms locked around me. But I don't feel caged by them. I feel protected.

"I want you to know Lori...I'm so proud of you for today. What you did was a huge step forward for you. You knew what you could handle, and you took it on like a champ. You faced your fears, and that's amazing."

"You...you really think so?"

"I do. I think you're so brave. I might not understand what it's like to be in your shoes, but you've been to hell and back. No one can measure their successes in the same way, least of all you. I don't care if other people think you've been hiding from the world. I think you've been taking time to recharge, and we all need that sometimes. I think you'll come out this end stronger than ever. And I admire you so much for that."

Vanessa wipes tears from my cheeks. I manage a smile, sniffing. I thought after everything we've endured, she'd want nothing to do with me. Or I thought maybe we'd stay friends, but she wouldn't be prepared to take on a relationship with me. But now I see that there's a reason Vanessa is perfect for me – she believes in me.

Now I just need to believe in myself.

AIRPORT

I sit shivering in the car even though the heater is on full blast. It's been a week since I took my first step out of the house, when I broke and ran all the way to Rococos to prove to myself that I could. The very next day, Wilda sat me down and told me that things were going to be different - I would start seeing a therapist immediately, I would take a month away from my studies, and I would call Marigold and tell her it was time for her to come home.

I knew deep in my heart that Wilda was right. And as she told me what I had to do, I saw a glimpse of Rita in her eyes. Just as I could never refuse Rita, I couldn't refuse Wilda.

It took me several days for me to work up the courage to call Marigold. Since she went away to Croatia, we haven't spoken much, and it's left a gaping hole in my heart. But when I called and told her she needed to come home, she booked a flight immediately. It almost made up for the fact that she left in the first place. But now, as I sit here stewing in anxiety, waiting for her plane to land, I wonder how I'll respond to seeing her.

Rowena refused to come with us to the airport. She's angrier with Marigold than anyone. I guess my anger took longer to come, but it's here now, making my chest feel hot. I know why she felt she had to go away, and from an unemotional standpoint, I wouldn't blame her. But now I think about what she left behind. Three daughters, two of them with abandonment issues, and all of them suffering from the same loss she felt. Not to mention that she has no idea what we've all been going through - my depression, Rowena's anger, and Honey's unhealthy studying habits. We were a mess when she left, and now we're a jigsaw puzzle that feels too broken to fit back together. She doesn't even know what she did when she left.

"It's okay," Wilda tells me, putting a hand on my knee. It's just the two of us waiting in the car. Honey opted not to come either, claiming her studies were more important. "I know you're angry with her. And that's okay."

I nod quietly. I'm glad that Wilda understands. My love for Marigold hasn't diminished in the slightest, but I don't trust her the way I used to. How can I when she made the decision to walk away when times got tough? I clench my hands in my lap. What could she possibly have achieved from going away that was more important than taking care of us?

When I see her rushing out of the terminal with her bags, I can barely even look at her. I forced myself out of the house thinking that I wanted to talk to her as soon as possible, that I was ready for a conversation about what she did, but now, the words have got lost in my mind, replaced only by bitter feelings. Marigold drops her bags by the car and rushes to my side of the vehicle to open the door and hug me, but I feel stiff in her arms as they envelop around me. She seems to realise that she's not receiving a warm welcome and pulls back from me, searching my face for an explanation.

"Lori…are you alright?" Her hand reaches out to touch my cheek. Can she feel beneath her fingertips how I've wasted away in the month she's been gone?

I turn to Wilda, not knowing what to say. Wilda offers me a sad smile.

"Maybe the two of you should catch up alone," Wilda offers. "I'll go and grab a quick bite to eat…then we can go home."

Home. I never imagined that I would call Wilda's house my home, but lately, it's started to feel like a place I could settle. Maybe simply because it's the only place I've known for months, but I don't feel any strong desire to leave there. Which is why it baffles me that Marigold can't see how odd it is that I'm not there. That I came all this way to meet her with anxiety weighing my chest down, and now I don't even want to speak to her. Why does she think I called her home? To have a picnic and a nice catch up?

I suddenly feel like I need air. I get out of the car and pace beside it while Marigold watches me with curiosity. After all, this is the first time she's seen me outside in months. But she's missed so much. I couldn't condense it all into a single sentence. And right now, what happened while she was gone only reminds me of the fact that I'm angry at her. I don't feel like I'm the one who owes an explanation.

"I can't believe you're here…my brave girl," Marigold says. I glare back at her. I hate the way that her skin is bronzed from the sun. I hate that there's a new tattoo peeping out from under her baggy clothing. I hate that someone has braided her short hair with coloured threads and that she looks better than she did even before Rita died. I should be glad to see that one of us is healing, but I'm not. Maybe that's selfish, but if her healing came at the cost of the rest of ours, then who is the selfish one here?

"I'm not brave. It took everything I have in me to come here today. Do you understand that at all?"

Marigold blinks several times, softening her face. "Yes…of course I do."

"But do you really? Do you know how hard it's been with you gone? How much we all wished you would've stayed?"

"But you…I thought you were okay with me leaving. I thought you understood why I was going."

"I do understand why you left. I know somewhere deep down you felt like it was the best thing to do. Maybe it was, for you. But we're a family. This isn't just about you. You just…you just left when things were at their worst and left a trail of destruction behind you. And none of us wanted to say anything, to stop you from doing what was best for yourself…but while we were thinking of you, did you think of any of us at all? You've barely even called."

"I…I thought I would give you the space to talk when you were all ready…"

"Because you understood that we were angry? If you knew then why did you go?"

"Lori, don't shout at me. I'm your mother-"

"Then act like it!" I snap. I regret it as soon as I say it, watching the hurt cross Marigold's face. She wraps her arms around herself, looking away from me with tears in her eyes.

"I've tried. I've always tried. But it never came so naturally to me," Marigold said, tears falling down her cheeks. "Rita was always the one you were all drawn to. The one you loved the most. And since she's been gone...I don't know how to fill that gap. I saw how you were drawn to Wilda, Lori. I saw how you settled better with her than you ever did with me. And I thought...I thought maybe that would make up for it all. That you'd be better off with Wilda anyway."

I take a step back from Marigold, feeling winded. I should've known that Marigold had this kind of insecurity of her place in our lives. Not many people can compare to Rita - the most enigmatic presence you'll ever have in your life, if you're lucky. But how could she turn away from her motherhood just because she felt second best? Especially because it isn't true?

"How can you say that? I...I care about Aunt Wilda very much. But she's not my mum. *You* are. You always have been. Which is why I can't just snap my fingers and forgive you for going away. This was your job. Your *only* job. I don't hate you for this. But I'm allowed to be angry."

Marigold is trembling now, her cheeks shining with tears. "Lori...I didn't know. I didn't know..."

I want to tell her to pull it together, but now isn't the moment. I step back toward her and reach for her hand. The rage inside me has dimmed just a little, and I need to connect with her. Healing from the burns this anger has caused inside me can wait. I have to let her know what's on my mind.

"You did know," I say quietly. "You *should* know. You made a big mistake...and it'll take time to fix it. But we all love you anyway. And I know that what you did you did out of love of your own. But Rita…she's gone. And she's not coming back. We're what's left. And you have to step up now."

Marigold's lip wobbles. "I know. I know. I'm so sorry, baby. I'm so sorry. I thought this would fix things. I thought I would get one last chance to be close to her again…but all that time out there…and I didn't feel her once."

"Mum…if she's anywhere, she's here. With her children, her sister, her wife. That's why we have to stay together. And you have to do better. That's all I'll ask of you. Just…just don't leave us again. Stay where you belong. Okay?"

"Okay," Marigold whispers. She pulls me into her chest and holds me hard. I don't want to hug her right now, but I also don't want to let go. She's all we have left. She smooths my hair down and kisses the top of my head.

"I'm sorry. I'm so sorry. And I'll never leave you again. I swear to you. I'll do everything I can to make this right again."

"We…we're going to need time."

She sniffs. "I know, baby, I know. But I won't give up. I'll make things right. No matter how long it takes."

Only now do I let my face rest against her shoulder. Because I believe her. I know her well enough to know that she'll fix this. How can I hold the only mistake she's ever made against her forever? As though I've been so perfect? Rowena and I came into her life like a hurricane and turned everything upside down, but she never gave up on us because of it. Life isn't perfect like a fairy story. I've lived enough nightmares to know that.

But there are slithers of gold to be found. And Marigold is mine.

RITA'S ROOM

Four months later…

It's been a while since I've been in a car. Months, in fact. The jittering of the engine beneath me makes me want to grip the seat and not let go, but it's a step forwards me even being in here – this is my first trip out of town in four months. It also happens to be our final trip home.

To Rita's old home.

Rowena's hand slides across the seat to find mine. I smile at her. I'm still getting used to seeing her without makeup. In recent months, she's ditched the black eyeliner and let her hair grow a little. She looks younger. She used to mask everything she might possibly be feeling. Now she seems exposed. She looks at me, her eyes a little watery.

"Do you think we'll be able to feel her there?" she asks. Her expression hardens. "I don't believe in ghosts.

I'm not a baby. I just…it was her home. It's going to be weird."

Honey reaches over my lap to grasp our entwined hands. "Don't worry so much, Ro. There's nothing to be scared of. If we feel her there, it's a good thing. It means she's still looking after us."

The comment seems to calm Rowena. It calms me too. Honey's always the voice of reason. Especially now that she's better settled at college. She came clean about her study drugs with my help shortly after Marigold came home from Croatia. Marigold and Wilda were furious, but they helped her through her exam period before insisting that she drop one of her subjects. Now, with summer exams coming up, she's nervous, but nowhere near as stressed as she was. We've both turned a corner in that respect.

Marigold turns around in her seat, smiling. Her face is a little more worn than a year ago, but she's still our Marigold. It took me a while before I could feel so warmly toward her again. But even after she left us, even after how much she hurt us, I knew I'd forgive her in time. Grief made idiots out of us all. I couldn't hold on to the things she'd done to grieve Rita.

"It's so nice to see you girls looking after each other," she says. Her hair has grown longer now, falling in wispy waves around her shoulders. We haven't talked much about the time that she was away, other than when she first came back. It seems like it was a darker time for us all. It's something probably best left in the past. Just like our old home.

Wilda sets off down our road. We're leaving here soon too. We're not the only ones deciding to leave a dark past behind. After the secrets I discovered in her attic, I can't blame Wilda for wanting to escape. The house is up for sale. We'll be moving to somewhere bigger to accommodate us all. Wilda coming with us doesn't even feel like an option. There's no way we're leaving her behind now.

The journey is quiet and nerve wracking. Wilda puts on one of Rita's old CDs and we all listen to her voice quietly humming just above the sound of the engine. Honey, Ro and I stay holding hands, and they both close their eyes to block out the journey, but I want to remember this. It feels like a turning point, and I don't want to forget the way I feel right now.

It's like deja vu as we enter our old neighbourhood. It takes a long time to drive through the busy market town, with traffic piling back for miles on end. We pass old restaurants where we used to eat sometimes, and the park where Honey played as she grew up. We pass the laundrette and the sets of small independent shops.

And then we turn left and we're on the street where it happened. I can see the pizza takeaway, its tacky lights flickering on and off as evening draws in. The lamppost where the car crashed into Rita has been replaced. I duck my head down between my legs. This is the one part of the journey I don't want to remember. Marigold strokes my head and I know she's crying too.

It's a relief when we escape the street where it happened. Rita's CD ends. We drive on in silence, pressure building on us each mile that we travel. This is it. There's no going back now.

The house looks the same on the outside. That surprises me for some reason. It feels like it should be crumbling and wasting away, destroyed by the death of Rita. The way we were. There's a for sale sign outside that the estate agents fixed up last week. We're here to take what's left of Rita's things. The furniture will be sold with the house. A new family will make memories here. Hopefully good ones.

The car stops on the driveway and we all sit in silence. Rowena titters nervously.

"This feels familiar."

It does. It's exactly like when we arrived at Wilda's house. Except now, her house feels more like home than here does. Marigold was right – we never could have stayed here. There are too many memories.

It feels good to be back in the house, though. It smells the same. Lavender still lingers in the air as we step inside. There are still remnants of Rita. Her beige coat still remains on its hook. Upstairs, her clothes are where we left them, piled on the chairs. I stepped over the threshold of this house wearing her old Timberland boots. It feels right. And I know where I want to go first.

"Do you guys mind if I go to her room?"

My family shake their heads, sending me on my way with encouraging words. I climb the stairs slowly, my hand dragging on the bannister. I see her bedroom at the end of the landing, the door slightly ajar, and I remember what Marigold told me. *When one door closes, another opens.* I guess she just wasn't quite ready to close the door on Rita the last time we were here.

When I flick the light on, Rita hits me like a cannonball. I should have remembered how much this room reflected her. And it's beautiful. I walk around it, touching everything on the chest of drawers, the vanity mirror, the bedside table. I sit on her bed, spotting several silver items on the bed. I scoop them into my hands, watching them settle on my palm. Rita's rings.

Someone knocks to come in. I look up and see Rowena's curious face peeping around the door. Honey stands behind her, rubbing goosebumps from her arms. I know how she feels. Being here is enough to make anyone feel cold.

Silently, the pair join me in the bedroom, sitting beside me on the bed. I show them the rings in my hands and Rowena immediately picks one out – a snake ring that engulfs two fingers at once, interweaving between the two. Rowena slides it on. It's a last reminder of her gothic days. It suits her slim fingers.

"You should keep it," Honey whispers to Ro. "Rita probably never told you what her rings meant to her…but she bought that ring soon after you moved in."

"Her favourite animal," Rowena says, lifting her hand to admire the snake. Honey nods.

"Exactly. And she picked it out for you. She had one for each of us."

She picks another ring from my palm. It's a gold band with tiny hexagons encircling it. Honey swallows, tears pricking her eyes as she puts it on.

"Honeycomb," she whispers. I look up and see that Wilda and Marigold are waiting by the door. I show them my palm.

"Which ones are yours?"

Marigold picks hers out with confidence. It's Rita's wedding band. Marigold slots it on her finger, right on top of her own wedding ring. It's a little big, but Mari doesn't seem to mind. She closes her fingers into her palm to keep it in place, smiling in content. Wilda scans my palm, less sure about her own ring. But then she spots one among them – a colourful piece with red roses and green vines twisting in and out.

"Wilderness," she mutters as she takes it. Rowena grins.

"Got to appreciate a good pun."

I smile, but I'm still looking for mine. A horrible feeling passes over me – that maybe she didn't have a ring for me. But Marigold picks one for me. She holds my hand and slips the ring on for me.

"A web. For delicacy and strength," she tells me. I examine the ring. It's the lightest of Rita's rings. Most of the others are made of heavy metals and are chunky to fit with her style. But this one is different. The band itself is slim, with the web weaved intricately out of delicate silver. Of all the things that have ever scared me, spiders were never one of them. Something Rita and I had in common. It's perfect.

We all sit for a while, admiring our rings. Marigold collects a few things together in a box. She doesn't take much. Just the important things. Rita's favourite sweater. Her leftover rings. Her guitar and her CDs. A few other items that mean something different to each of us. Each a show of her strength, or her beauty, or her never-ending kindness. Things we'll look back on with broken hearts and a smile on our face. Rita was everything. Even now she's gone, she still matters so much. She's still what holds us all together.

Honey leaves the room first. I suspect she's gone to find a quiet place to mourn. Rowena follows her, twirling her new ring around her fingers with pride. Wilda kisses our cheeks and promises to meet us outside. She takes the box of Rita's things with her. Then it's just Marigold and I left. Mari takes my hand and we sit for a while on the bed, looking around the room.

"This is it," Marigold says. I lean my head against her shoulder.

"I know."

Marigold sniffs, smoothing the duvet with her free hand. "I think…I think this is the hardest thing I'll ever do."

I nod, unable to speak for the tightness in my throat.

"But it'll be better now, won't it? We're getting better."

I squeeze her hand. "Better every day."

She nods. I stand up, pulling Marigold to her feet. She hugs me close and I thank God that I still have her. And Wilda, and Honey, and Ro. Vanessa too. But right now is a time to be thankful for family – even when Rita is gone forever.

We leave the room hand in hand. Marigold's breathing is shaky as we stand outside, taking one last look at the room. Marigold wavers, her hand on the doorknob. She bites her lip, tears trickling down her cheeks. I squeeze her hand.

"It's okay," I tell her. Marigold nods, scrunching her eyes closed and releasing more tears. But her hand is steady beneath mine.

Together, we pull the door closed.

ABOUT THE AUTHOR

HAYLEY ANDERTON is a full time ghostwriter and the author of the YA LGBT romance novel, Double Bluff. She is also the co-author of the Kindle Unlimited series, Apocalypse. When she's not writing she loves to bake and hang out with fluffy friends. For editing services and business enquiries, she can be contacted at hayleyandertonbusiness@gmail.com.

Instagram: @hayley_a_writes
Twitter: @handerton96
Wattpad: @hazzer123

If you enjoyed this novel, please consider reviewing it on Amazon and Goodreads! Reviews can make or break an indie author's career, so any thoughts you have are much appreciated!

Printed in Great Britain
by Amazon